THE PYRAMID & THE PAINTING

THE PYRAMID & THE PAINTING

KAYT C. PECK

SAPPHIRE BOOKS

SALINAS, CALIFORNIA

Sapphire Books Publishing, LLC
P.O. Box 8142
Salinas, CA 93912
www.sapphirebooks.com

Printed in the United States of America
First Edition – June 2018

This and other Sapphire Books titles can be found at
www.sapphirebooks.com

Dedication

To my friends and neighbors in the village of Rociada, New Mexico. Your lives inspire me.

Acknowledgments

To Sapphire Books for giving my work a public voice and for their whole team of "sisters" who believe in the power of the written word. I find myself in prestigious company and am proud to be one of them.

Prologue

Kidwell watched as the brown liquid dribbled from the coffee maker into the pot. On the counter beside it were two cold biscuits, halved and each with a smear of peanut butter and a squirt of honey. The biscuits could wait. She craved that coffee. Milk and sugar already rested at the bottom of her favorite mug - the thick, ceramic one with the US Navy seal on the side – the one she'd bought in the Pentagon uniform supply shop. As she watched and waited for the coffee, she did the math in her head. The hefty mug had been her companion for twenty-six years.

Sometimes she missed the "cowboy" coffee they'd made over an ancient wood stove in a chipped and dented enamel pot when she, her wife, Anna, and their best friends, Aisha and Greg, had spent months in heavenly exile at Thunder Lake, a sacred site of the Taos Pueblo tribe. That time in hiding with few comforts, living in a ramshackle shack and teepees, had been one of the best times of her life.

All their lives were changed forever when Kidwell and Aisha became reluctant mystics and prophets, Kidwell in the kiva cave at Bandelier National Monument and Aisha at a vandalized mosque. White Buffalo Calf Woman came to Kidwell, and Kadijah, first wife of the Prophet Mohammed, came to Aisha. Each woman received messages for the world, messages that would draw the wrath of the powerful. A warning from her former commander and dear friend, Admiral John O'Hare, told of those who would come for them – and so the four ran to the mountains, mystical magic leading them to relative safety at Thunder Lake.

When the danger passed, from both the physical and the mystic world, Kidwell and Anna came home – home to their cabin in the woods, but life would never be the same. While in exile, they had written *The Book of Kidwell* and *The Book of Aisha*, passing on the lessons given by their spirit guides. Unplanned, the books spread. People from throughout much of the world consumed those books like a starving man finding a loaf of bread. Like it or not, hordes now viewed Kidwell and Aisha as prophets, perhaps saviors of humanity. Kidwell wore the mantel with reluctance and discomfort, but she was never one to shirk her duty, whatever that may be.

The coffee finally finished brewing, and Kidwell poured a cup greedily. She took a long drink before stepping away from the counter, closing her eyes with the pleasure of that first hit of caffeine. She topped off the cup before taking mug in one hand and plate in the other and heading from the kitchen to her office. She would eat at her desk. Anna slept soundly still. Kidwell tried to address the most urgent "prophet" matters before her lover awoke each morning.

Admiral O'Hare, now retired, had become the manager of the multitude of demands imposed upon these modern prophets. While a carefully selected staff viewed the hundreds of letters and emails received each day, a special few were selected for decisions by Kidwell or Aisha themselves. As Kidwell set the plate on her desk, taking another long gulp of coffee, she saw the fat, brown envelope that Martin, the young

Apache who was her assistant and guardian, had left for her to open. She felt a tingle, a certainty that today, there was truly something important awaiting her. As she slit the envelope open, a magic light glowed from within. She had seen that light before. Kidwell emptied the contents onto her desk, and there she could see that the light came from one battered and weather-stained envelope. She picked it up and looked at the return address. It came from a convent in southern Mexico.

"Open it." She heard a whisper behind her. She recognized the voice of White Buffalo Calf Woman.

Kidwell sighed as she looked at the glowing envelope in her hand.

Oh dear, here we go again, she thought.

Chapter One

Failure and Opportunity

This is different," Kidwell Brown said to no one in particular. Just as well that she spoke to no one because there was no one to speak to for at least fifty miles. She was as alone as she had ever been in her life. Unless, of course, one counted the spider monkeys scurrying through the tree canopy above along with the hordes of colorful birds, none of which Kidwell could name. Then there was the distinct and bone chilling call of the jaguar she had heard barely an hour into her hike through the thick jungle after leaving behind her Mayan driver and guide.

She had hiked the Rocky and Smoky Mountains, traveled the High Plains, and known life on the high seas. She had traversed the deserts of the Southwest and even the deserts of the Middle East while serving in Desert Storm. She knew well how to survive in a wilderness, but this jungle was, indeed, different. It was an alien world for her.

Her Mayan guide had begged her not to go, even after he had seen the miracle of the map that had brought them as far as roads could take them. He feared for her life, and her soul. He knew Kidwell, the prophet of whom he had heard and the woman he had grown to call friend during her weeks striving to bring peace to his troubled homeland. He had stayed close to her, assigned by the Mother Superior of his village convent, to serve as her protector during Kidwell's time there after Kidwell answered the Mother Superior's call for help. The man had watched Kidwell's broken Spanish improve over the weeks, and her mission of peace fail. He had grown to believe in her, despite that failure.

The Mayan had watched Kidwell's fruitless efforts at a miracle. For weeks, Kidwell had pursued every lead, asked every person, knelt in prayer with the humble people of the village, all the while begging for a meeting with the drug lord who was dictator as much as criminal. The man held enough territory, weapons, men, and power that not even *federales* could touch him. The people suffered from his wanton cruelty and the way in which he took whatever he wanted from a people so poor that they could not spare what he took. The women he captured, adding sexual slavery to his many crimes, paid perhaps the highest price of all.

Finally, the drug lord's men had come in the night, taking Kidwell from her bed, blindfolding her and granting her wish to meet with the drug lord. As Kidwell walked into his opulent lair, she smelled the familiar stench of evil, one she had known before as she battled a man possessed by an evil soul, a battle that would have taken her life if not for the gift of a blessed sword given her by her spirit guides. The meeting ended before it even began, with the drug lord's laugh after he spit in her face, interrupting her pleas for the people. He had ordered her beaten and killed, but his men were frightened. They had heard the stories of Kidwell the Prophet. Instead, they had taken her to a dark place, a dangerous place, leaving her fate in the hands of nature. Blindfolded and bound, rough hands lifted Kidwell from the bed of a truck where she rode, bruised and jostled, and then they dropped her and sent her rolling down an embankment. The hiss of snakes greeted her when she finally came to a stop, hearing the roar of the truck engine as the men drove away.

Winded and disoriented, Kidwell waited for the sting of the first bite. She waited to die.

Something happened. She felt rather than saw a presence, a vibration of energy familiar to her, one that meant the presence of a spirit being. Blindfolded, she had no clue who the being might be, but relief replaced the depth of a cold and all-consuming fear. The hiss of snakes and the cacophony of the jungle were gone, replaced with the familiar sounds of a village. She felt hands untie the ropes around her wrists and ankles, and arms lift her, setting her gently down before removing the blindfold. Kidwell opened her eyes to see the familiar village plaza of the town that was her temporary home. Her rescuer was gone, and Kidwell didn't question. She'd learned to simply accept the gift of magic.

After a brief rest from her trauma in the humble room that was her temporary home, the map arrived. Kidwell knew then what her next step must be.

"*Necessito vamos,*" Kidwell said, standing outside the door of the Mayan's humble home after awakening him in the early hours of a quiet morning. When the man asked why and where they must go, "*Ahora!*" was the only answer he received. The cold blue of her eyes and the set expression on her face convinced him that when she said, "Now," she meant just that. He was not one to argue with a prophet.

On the map they followed, the road glowed with an eerie light, one that guided them out of the village and toward sparsely populated areas on roads rarely traveled. For hours, they bumped and banged in his ancient pickup along rutted tracks, all the while following the glowing trail on the map Kidwell held, one unlike any the Mayan had ever seen. In Spanish, he asked where she got it.

"From White Buffalo Calf Woman," she answered.

The Mayan's eyes widened. He had read parts of the Spanish translation of the *Book of Kidwell* and the *Book of Aisha*, accounts of the early days when Kidwell and her dear friend, Aisha, had been called as prophets. He knew about White Buffalo Calf Woman as a holy messenger. He reached to touch the map reverently, thinking as he did so that he might as well touch the original roses given by Our Lady of Guadalupe to Juan Diego in 1531. His hand shook with the revelation that he played a small role in great events.

When the track ended, and they could drive no farther, the light from the map faded and a glowing orb appeared, hovering beside a footpath into the jungle.

"I go alone from here, my friend," Kidwell said in Spanish.

"Please, dear lady, this is a dangerous place. There are old spirits as well as the jaguar. Do not go."

Kidwell motioned toward the hovering orb. "I cannot ignore such a call."

Tears appeared in the Mayan's eyes. "*Vaya con Dios,*" he answered.

Kidwell smiled, answering in Spanish. "Is there any other way to go?"

She hefted her pack from the back of the truck, checking her water supply and general condition of the pack she'd brought with her from her home in New Mexico. She shouldered the heavy pack, and waved a sad goodbye to the man who had been her protector and friend.

The Mayan watched until he could see no sign of her through the dense growth. The map was on the seat beside him, glowing once again, showing him the road home. The Mayan wept in earnest, touched that a holy messenger would remember to show him the way back. When he got home, he would give the map to the Mother Superior. She would know what to do with such a holy object.

❧❧❧❧❧

Kidwell continued her walk in the muggy heat. She watched mosquitoes the size of hummingbirds – or so it seemed to her – fly around her. She knew not whether it was the insect repellent bracelet she wore or the protective hand of her spirit guides that kept her safe from their potentially deadly bite. The white orb continued to float before her, leading her ever deeper into the jungle. For a moment, as they topped a rise, there was a break in the overgrowth, and Kidwell could see into the distance. Three, perhaps four miles ahead, she saw the distinct mounds in the jungle that she had come to know as the hidden remains of Mayan and Aztec pyramids and structures long forgotten. She saw also the flattened shadows of a rapidly setting sun. She felt a twinge of apprehension at the thought of walking through a darkened jungle, followed quickly by the longing of homesickness she had felt so often during her weeks in the Yucatan.

Anna, she thought longingly, wishing desperately for the comforting presence of her lover. She closed her eyes and imagined the depths of Anna's dark eyes, and smelling the sweetness of her breath, her skin.

Kidwell shook her head, bringing her mind back to this place, this moment. She noticed that the white orb had stopped its progress and floated up the trunk of an angled tree to a wide pocket in a branch of that tree. Kidwell realized that the orb was guiding her to a haven of rest for the night. The thought of rest increased the ache of her feet and her shoulders where they bore the brunt of the weight of her pack. Carefully, Kidwell used both hands to help herself up the trunk of the steeply angled tree.

When she reached the orb, it hovered above a perfect pocket where three huge branches met. It was just the right size for Kidwell in her sleeping bag. She would simply drape the shell of her one-person tent over her, providing protection from the rain likely to come during the night. She pulled from her pack a meal of fruit and nut bars with a small can of chicken salad with crackers and then drank long and deep from the water bladder in her pack. Carefully, she rinsed the empty can and then packed the remains of the meal into an airtight trash-bag.

Kidwell looked at the monkeys scattered in the trees around her. She laughed.

"Don't guess hanging a bear bag will do much good here," she said to herself.

"Those little suckers would be into it in a minute." In New Mexico, the next camp chore would be to secure all food and trash a distance from the camp and hung well out of reach of any bear.

She was concerned for her own safety as well as that of her food. Kidwell reached for the 9-mm pistol in the holster on her belt. The village constable loaned her the weapon when she first arrived. She missed her .357, but the cold steel of the automatic still comforted her. While, in her life, she fought for peace, Kidwell was at her core a warrior for that peace.

"Do not worry," a voice said, a voice that sounded more like bells than flesh. "I shall watch over you."

Kidwell looked above. The white orb was gone. In its place was a man, beautiful of face and dressed in white. No, not dressed in white but covered in white light.

"Do I know you?" she asked.

"You have always known me," he answered.

In her heart, she felt he was right. "Do I know your name?"

"Is there any need?" He smiled. Once again, the angel became an orb.

Kidwell laughed, suddenly very much at home in this strange jungle. She left her gear in the nook of the tree and scrambled to the bottom where she urinated, right at the base of the tree. In addition to the angel's protection, she hoped the scent of human would discourage predators.

Once back in her safe-haven, boots off and wrapped in sleeping bag and tent, Kidwell was asleep before the last light of the sun faded for the day. She dreamed, although in the four years since her vision at the cave kiva of Bandelier National Monument, it was sometimes difficult for her to know dreams from reality. Kidwell expected a restless night in the oppressive humidity of the jungle surrounded by the unfamiliar night sounds of insects whose depth of voice matched the size of these super bugs. Instead, she slept peacefully in the pocket of her tree haven, dreaming of the sweet scent of pine trees from her mountain home and the comforting warmth of Anna beside her. The recurring dream sustained her through her self-imposed exile in the Yucatan.

When Kidwell felt a gentle pressure against her face, she smiled in half-sleep and reached up to pet Milagra, their cat and the loving creature who frequently served as a furry alarm clock. A sensation such as she'd never known before greeted her fingers instead of familiar, soft fur. It was as though she touched light – warm and pure – as though what her eyes saw in the morning sun suddenly transformed into a tactile sensation. There was more. There was, well, goodness in the touch. She felt as comforted as an infant in the arms of a loving parent. Despite the surrounding jungle with all its hazards and unfamiliarity, in that instant Kidwell felt as loved and safe as she had ever felt in her life. Kidwell's eyes opened and she stared directly at the orb of light that had guided her the prior day. It hovered near her face, and Kidwell was surprised that she had slept through the night, the morning sun already fully above the horizon.

"Time to go?" Kidwell asked. The orb did not respond. "Time enough for coffee?" The orb floated to a nearby branch and rested peacefully.

Kidwell sat up and realized that a rain in the night had pooled water in the pockets of the tent shell she had draped over herself and her pack. She used the rainwater to rinse her face and hands and run moisture through her night-tangled hair. After spreading the tent over a branch to dry, Kidwell rummaged in her pack for comb, toothbrush, camp stove, and coffee bags. It took only a few minutes to heat coffee and make a breakfast of trail-mix. She felt amazingly rested, and needed the coffee to aid her brain into wakefulness. Frankly, it was the best she'd felt since leaving New Mexico.

As she savored the hot, sweet coffee, two spider

monkeys dropped to the branch where the orb rested. The monkeys huddled together, obviously chattering to one another about the strange object. Tendrils of light snaked out of the orb, nearly touching the monkeys and then slipping abruptly back into the orb whenever one of the primates made to touch the finger of light. Kidwell laughed at the playful show, and she was certain she heard the tinkle of bells from the orb, suspecting as she did that it was angel laughter.

The last of the coffee consumed, Kidwell checked the water in her drinking bladder and water bottles. She'd need to stop soon at one of the many water-filled sinkholes for refills. Hopefully, her purification pump with chlorine drops intended for Rocky Mountain streams was adequate for the microorganisms of the life-rich jungle.

Kidwell made short work of replacing stove, cup, sleeping bag, and tent in her pack. Once she was trail ready once again, she gently dropped her pack to the ground and scurried down the tree, where, at the base, she urinated in the same place she had the night before.

"Thank you, tree," she said, her hand resting on the trunk. For a moment, she felt a flow of energy beneath her fingers. The tree heard her gratitude.

When Kidwell shouldered her pack, and turned her attention to the trail, the orb was waiting for her. She smiled a greeting at the being she knew was within and followed. As she had the evening before, Kidwell looked through an opening in the thick growth and saw in the distance the mounds of earth and vegetation, which she knew to mean the buried remains of a dead civilization. Throughout her journey from the village to the tree, Kidwell had sublimated any curiosity she felt at this newest quest assigned her by White Buffalo

Calf Woman. Kidwell learned long ago that she would know what she needed to know when she needed to know it. As she looked toward the distant mounds once again, Kidwell felt an unexplained excitement, an eagerness to reach her goal, whatever that may be.

The orb started to vibrate. Kidwell suspected it was the angelic equivalent of patting its foot impatiently. Kidwell walked.

Jungle surrounded her as it had the day before and mile after mile passed under her feet, the orb guiding her way. Kidwell began to understand some of the cycles of life around her in the unfamiliar jungle. It became easier to visually separate the snakes, spiders, and frogs camouflaged in the undergrowth, and she began to hear the nuances of communication in the chattering of the monkeys that followed her progress from their vantage points in the canopy of the trees. Oddly, her surroundings changed. The trees became fewer and the path well-tended and marked with lines of stone. She tried to remember the map, but she did not recall anything resembling a civilized community in the area. Then she started to see the raised gardens, immaculately kept and rich with produce.

The first people she saw were as much of a surprise to her as she was to them. They had the familiar regal beauty in face and body of the indigenous people she had grown to love in the village, but the dress was unfamiliar, more like something from the paintings in the museums of Mexico City rather than that of indigenous *peones.* Without exception, they stopped work in the gardens to stare at Kidwell and her orb companion, and one older man whispered to a youth working with him. The youth jumped to the ground and ran down the path at break-neck speed.

Kidwell tripped over nothing, as she forgot her feet, amazed at the sights around her. The prophet knew that somehow, she was walking into a city, as it had been a millennium or more earlier. She heard the tinkle of bells and strongly suspected that her orb guide was having a good laugh at her expense.

Surprise became mind-boggling amazement as Kidwell rounded a corner and saw the city, a massive chalk-white pyramid at its heart. There were people everywhere. Every structure was magnificently built and covered in stark-white plaster with bright murals adding color to every public building. A game court had a prominent place in the city, and blocks of structures provided homes for hundreds of the people who filled streets and the ever-present raised gardens scattered throughout the city. As she walked, people stopped to stare in stunned silence when she passed. The cacophony of a covered market could be heard from a distance, but all chatter stopped once Kidwell and the orb came within sight.

A phalanx of feathered and leather-covered warriors stood in Kidwell's path as she and the orb rounded a corner. The spears, bows, and arrows they carried looked as beautiful as they did deadly. Kidwell took a deep breath, trying to steady her knees as she approached the fearsome men and one woman. As they drew close, the orb stopped and hovered before Kidwell.

"You're going to leave me now, aren't you?" Kidwell asked her guide.

She heard the tinkle of bells and then, within the confines of her own mind, a lyrical voice said, "I am always with you."

With a loud pop and the smell of lavender,

the orb disappeared, causing the warriors to jump, taking a fighting stance. Kidwell found one spear-tip dangerously near her throat. She put her hands before her, palms up.

"Believe me, I'm no threat," she said, giving a shaky smile.

The warriors held their spears in slightly more relaxed positions, but still at the ready. Two of them, the leaders, Kidwell assumed, talked together, arguing. Kidwell didn't understand, but she heard the musical flow of the language she'd heard the villagers use among themselves, saving Spanish or English for their conversations with her and the nuns of the convent.

The argument lasted only moments, before a short, stocky man, the oldest of the group, stepped before her, the butt of his spear resting on the ground. He looked Kidwell in the eye and spoke with a voice of authority.

"I don't understand," she answered.

In a fluid motion, using his spear as a pointer, the man made it clear Kidwell was to follow him. The warriors made a column on each side of her, and Kidwell continued her walk through the city. They set a pace somewhat more than she wanted after her two-day hike, but she didn't feel that it was up for discussion. She managed to keep up, but by the time they led her to the base of the pyramid at the center of the city, she was sweating profusely and breathing hard.

An elderly man was sitting in the shade of a tree beside the pyramid. He was dressed in simple white robes with a leather band, stained turquois, around his head. The man waved the warriors away, despite protest from the leader of the squad. Once they were alone together, the man offered her a seat on the bench, and dipped a gourd cup into an earthen jar of fresh water beside the bench. He offered Kidwell the cup and she drank deeply some of the sweetest water she had ever consumed, water with a hint of mint and maybe chamomile.

The man spoke at length in the Mayan – or she assumed it was Mayan – language. The only word she understood was "Quetzacoatl." She knew the name of the feathered serpent god, and she felt a knot of fear. There were mixed reviews in the legends of that being, many of them tied with tales of human sacrifice. The man, a priest, Kidwell assumed, repeatedly referred to Quetzacoatl and pointed up the long stairs to the top of the pyramid. The message was clear. Kidwell was to meet a god. She wished she'd had an opportunity to shower first.

Once she had rested, the priest stood and led the way. Kidwell had placed her pack beside the bench. She shouldered it once again and followed the man, resisting the urge to count what seemed like an infinite number of steps. If she had known what the day would bring, she would have stopped for an early lunch. Kidwell was grateful for the age of her guide. Even though she was astounded at how easily the elderly man traversed the steps, she knew she could not have kept pace with her earlier warrior guides, not without risking a heart attack. When they were nearly three-quarters of the way to the top, the priest stopped and turned to look behind them; he smiled and pointed with pride at the city below. Kidwell turned to follow his gaze and became breathless from more than the climb. The city was magnificent. Buildings were consistently stark white against the green backdrop of the jungle, and gardens throughout the city added to the color of murals on the walls of public buildings. Kidwell had read theories about Mayan cities and how they had made a rich living from terraced gardens created from the muck of the many jungle wetlands. The theories were true.

They finished the long climb, and Kidwell stepped within the walled area that surrounded the flat top of the pyramid. At the center was a dais with a throne, and standing there was a creature, the sight of which made it hard for Kidwell to breathe. He truly was a winged serpent, three times the size of a large man. The golden scales were so shiny, they reflected the sunlight, and colorful feathers covered the wings at rest on his back. The head was massive, with a bright intelligence reflected in the eyes.

"Do you fear me?" the god asked in Mayan, but Kidwell's mind heard it in clear English.

"Of course," she answered. Kidwell looked to her right, and saw that the priest had knelt, his forehead resting on the stone. Kidwell bent her knees but hesitated.

"Do not bow," the god said. "You are not one of my subjects."

In an odd visual flow, the winged serpent transformed, morphing into that of a tall and regal man, with a golden covering from waist to knee that perfectly replicated the scales of the serpent and a huge, feathered headdress that included the colors of his wings.

"Remember what you just saw," he said. "It will be important that you know it is possible."

"I don't understand," Kidwell responded. He ignored her.

"So, you think you can serve my people?" he demanded, a note of derision in his voice.

"I tried," Kidwell answered. "I failed."

The god strode from the dais and stood towering before her. "Not yet, you haven't. And I fully expect that you shall not. You must not," he said.

Kidwell held her ground, knowing that this was no time to show fear, but she seriously wished she had the option of peeing her pants. He was terrifying. She heard a quiet sound behind the god, a clearing of a throat. The god stood perfectly still.

"This is not the time, Sister," he said sternly.

"It most certainly is," a gentle voice answered in Mayan, another voice who Kidwell's mind heard in clear English.

The god turned, no longer blocking Kidwell's view of the dais. There stood a woman who equaled or excelled her brother in stature and beauty. She wore a feathered headdress as well, and a white, close fitting gown accented in gold.

"I am Tonantzin," the goddess said. "We welcome you to our lands, Kidwell the Prophet."

"I am honored," Kidwell answered, feeling the same energy, the same magnetism she felt when in the presence of White Buffalo Calf Woman.

The goddess stepped from the dais and held out her hand to Kidwell. "Come, I have much to tell you."

"I am not finished," Quetzacoatl said.

The goddess laughed and touched her brother's arm playfully. "She knows you are terrifying and that she must not fail. She has seen the nature of who you are. What more is there, my brother?"

The stern face of the god softened. His sister obviously had the power to soothe his fearsome nature.

"Perhaps you are right, Sister. It would be best if you told her what more she must know of us to give her—" His voice cracked with emotion. "—to revive the great gifts we once imparted on our people." Kidwell was surprised to see the depth of his emotion.

"Come," the goddess said, turning once again to Kidwell.

Kidwell followed the goddess as she walked across the top of the pyramid to a door on one side of the wall. It did not look as if there was space for a room behind that door in the relatively narrow stone wall, but Kidwell followed. The goddess opened the door and led the way inside. As soon as she stepped through the opening, Kidwell found herself not atop a pyramid, but in a tropical paradise, including waterfall and gentle lagoon. The sight and smell of roses wafted everywhere. The goddess continued to lead the way, and as she walked, she morphed into the familiar shape of a blue robed saint, Our Lady of Guadalupe. The goddess morphed again, taking on her original aspect.

"So, who are you?" Kidwell asked. "Tonantzin or Our Lady of Guadalupe?"

The goddess laughed and turned to face Kidwell. "I took the form needed to save my people. It was not a hard thing to do. Mary did not mind that I borrowed her shape, her name. She was relieved I found a way to lessen the damage of the misguided followers of her son."

"Hello," Kidwell heard a voice call. She looked toward the sound and saw White Buffalo Calf Woman waiting for them, sitting on a buffalo robe spread near the lagoon. Food and drink were spread on the robe, presenting a lovely picnic. Kidwell laughed. Aisha, her fellow prophet, had told her of her visits with Khadija and Mohammed and the lovely food they provided. Kidwell looked forward to getting to know White Buffalo Calf Woman in a whole new way.

"Welcome, Kidwell," White Buffalo Calf Woman said.

"Thank you so much," Kidwell responded. At the sight of the food, her stomach growled, and the two goddesses laughed musically. Tonantzin drifted gracefully to sit on the robe. Kidwell dropped her pack, and took her own place there.

White Buffalo Calf Woman held out a covered platter of simple stoneware. "Here, I know you have missed these."

Kidwell took the dish and removed the cover. Underneath was an exact replica of the *chili relleno* plate from her favorite New Mexican restaurant. Refried beans, *posole,* and a still hot *sopapilla* with honey finished the meal. Kidwell ate as though she hadn't eaten in years, fighting back the tickle of tears in her eyes at the familiar flavors. All that was missing was Anna to keep her company. As Kidwell thought of Anna, White Buffalo Calf Woman placed her hand on Kidwell's arm, looking deep into her eyes.

"Be strong," the goddess said. "It will all be as it should in the end."

"I don't understand," Kidwell responded.

"You will," the goddess answered.

Kidwell did not question. She learned long ago that she would not receive an answer until it was time.

All three ate and laughed, and the goddesses acted like old friends, telling stories to each other that Kidwell only half understood. When the meal was done, Tonantzin rose gracefully, and held out her hand to Kidwell.

"It is time for you to go," the goddess said.

"I will see you again," White Buffalo Calf Woman added.

Kidwell took Tonantzin's offered hand and rose. She shouldered her pack, waved to the still seated Lakota spirit woman, and followed the Mayan goddess away from their picnic. White Buffalo Calf Woman waved a hand, and the entire remains of their picnic disappeared.

"I must ask you to take something back with you," Tonantzin said.

"Of course, I will," Kidwell answered.

"Do you remember the earthen jar Peter brought you?"

"Certainly," Kidwell said. "It was when we were all in hiding at Thunder Lake near Taos Pueblo. The Apostle Peter came, and he left us a large earthen jar. When we opened it, it held the entire Nag Hammadi library in perfect condition. Impossibly, hundreds of mint condition ancient scrolls came out of that jar. Scholars are still sorting through it all."

"Would you do the same for my people?" the goddess asked.

"What is that?"

"Save what never should have been lost?"

Kidwell smiled. "Of course, if it is in my power."

The goddess waved her hand and an earthen jar appeared, mounted on a rough, wheeled cart. "Then take this back with you."

Kidwell looked at it, perplexed. "I would die trying, but I'm not sure I have the strength to get this through the jungle."

The goddess laughed. "There is no need." She waved her hand and another door appeared. "Thank you, Kidwell Brown, for fighting to save my people. It is time for you to go, but I must tell you one more thing."

"Yes?"

"When you are given power to win the battles, do not forget that it is more important to win the war."

"I don't understand."

"You will." The goddess lifted the ancient leather and wood latch on the door, opening it. Kidwell could only see bright sunlight on the other side. "Goodbye, Kidwell Brown. Know that we are watching and will help when we can."

"I am honored to have met you, and I will do what I can for the Maya."

"I know," the goddess answered.

Kidwell grasped the handle on the cart and pulled the earthen jar through the door. There was a moment of vertigo once she and the cart had cleared the doorway, and Kidwell found herself standing in the dirt street outside the home of her Mayan guide and friend. The man sat on a bench beside his front door, a cool drink in a pottery cup beside him. He looked surprised at her sudden appearance, but quickly recuperated, laughing in joy and calling for his wife and children to greet their guest. Kidwell was smothered in hugs and laughter from the family and from the neighbors who heard the commotion. She learned quickly that the entire village had assumed she was dead.

In time, they lifted the lid of the earthen jar and peeked inside. Mayan codices filled it. Kidwell cried and laughed. Centuries of lost knowledge would now be regained. She made plans with her friend, taking preliminary steps to ship the precious jar and its contents to the university in Mexico City.

Her friend's wife insisted Kidwell come inside for a meal, but Kidwell graciously declined. She was still too full of *rellenos*.

Chapter Two

The Eyes of an Artist

Greg, her husband, slept peacefully beside her, but Aisha stared open-eyed at the ceiling. Trouble was, she didn't see the ceiling. The vision had awakened her from a sound sleep, and it compelled her, making her hands itch for brush and canvas. This would not go away. Aisha knew this was more than simple inspiration. It was a calling as surely as if the spirit of Khadija, the Prophet Mohammad's first and well-beloved wife, had taken Aisha by the hand and led her to the canvas. Khadija often provided Aisha with guidance, but not this night. As Aisha lie awake, she saw a scene and people far outside any life experience she'd ever know, physical or spiritual. Still, she knew it to be real and as critical to paint as the vision of Hermit's Peak given her by Khadija. That painting made it possible for her to first meet Kidwell, her friend, her fellow prophet.

Aisha carefully slipped from under the sleeping embrace of her gently snoring husband. Not bothering to put a robe over her pajamas, Aisha shuffled through the darkened house, taking care not to make unnecessary noise or stub a toe. When she got to her studio at the far side of the house, she flipped on the light switch and repositioned directional lights around her easel to make up for the lack of daylight. This painting wouldn't wait for sunrise. She pulled a large, blank canvas from a rack, squeezed her usual selection of colors on her well-used pallet, and went to work, making first a quick outline sketch in charcoal.

She worked like a woman possessed, painting an alien world with vegetation with as much blue as green, and a home cut into the side of a mountain, with bluish grass on walls and roof. As she painted, she saw even greater detail in the vision before her eyes, and she found herself fully focused on minute details such as large and long serrated leaves on the equivalent of trees, with each leaf being its own branch. As she turned to the rich blue of the sky, she saw a sun with a deep, blue tone to its light, and, on the horizon, one moon hung above the line of mountains and a second, the larger of the two, just peeking over the ridge.

☙ ☙ ❧ ❧

Sometime after the sun finally rose, Greg stumbled sleepily into the studio, a coffee mug in each hand. Aisha paused only briefly to look at him with grateful eyes and take the cup, downing the coffee nearly in a single gulp, leaving a smear of cadmium blue on the cup handle.

She returned immediately to painting. Greg watched for a few minutes as she completed clouds with odd splotches of orange amid the bluish-white. Aisha simply painted what she saw, not having a clue about the science behind this atmospheric anomaly. Greg left her to work, returning a few minutes later to place a plate with a hardboiled egg and sliced mango as well as a glass of ice water on the table beside her. He hoped she'd see it. He worried about his wife when a painting truly obsessed her, and what he saw coming to life on the canvas mystified him.

Greg left the studio, heading for his own office. He had a busy day ahead. True, he only taught part-time as an adjunct now. He had grown to accept being the spouse of a prophet, including the reality of the business and operational side. Aisha got the messages from the spirit realm, but Greg opened the mail, and there was lots of mail. Without any requests for support, hundreds of thousands of dollars came in as unsolicited gifts and thousands of copies of *The Book of Kidwell* and *The Book of Aisha* were purchased every day. Greg had been grateful when Kidwell's dear friend, retired Admiral O'Hare, had offered to form the nonprofit corporation that now handled the business end of being a prophet. Neither Kidwell nor Aisha had been comfortable with the profit side of prophesying, but they quickly realized that the demands were such that it was impossible to maintain a normal life, including the daily task of making a living. Kidwell took little, instead continuing to rely on her retirement from the Navy, although she did allow the nonprofit to cover her costs of travel and supplement her income if needed. Aisha and Greg had both given up their full-time faculty positions, and Kidwell was the one who insisted that the nonprofit pay them at the same level as their former salaried positions. Still, the money came unsolicited. Within a year of forming the nonprofit, Admiral O'Hare suggested that they also form a private foundation which now made sizeable grants to groups throughout the world struggling to improve the human condition, sometimes fighting hunger, disease, injustice – the nasty, warty side of humanity, and sometimes funding visions of what could be – the arts, community development. Greg worked with the Admiral sometimes. It was good work, and helped ease the occasional longing for his days doing research on water issues on the arid High Plains, and instilling a love for science in his students. Then Aisha had quietly insisted that the foundation fund an extra special project – Greg's research. With the extra funding, he made great strides in understanding the recharge process that maintained the massive Ogallala Aquifer that hydrated humanity in parts of five states. He continued to work with the University, now aided by a platoon of graduate students and post-docs.

Greg settled in at his desk. First, he would check emails the nonprofit forwarded to Aisha. The clerical staff initially reviewed them, with those needing personal attention forwarded as appropriate to Aisha and Greg or to Kidwell and Anna. Greg's brow creased. They were all worried about Kidwell, somewhere in the Yucatan for over two months, communication from her infrequent and brief. He'd begun to worry also that Anna's emails and calls were becoming less frequent and somehow veiled. He would be relieved when Kidwell was safely in New Mexico. At times, he felt he should have gone with her. When the four of them had been exiles at Thunder Lake, he and Kidwell were the guardians, the protectors. More and more, Kidwell faced alone the hazardous adventures, the requests for help from people in a troubled world. He hated that his friend faced it alone, without him, Anna, or Aisha by her side. There had been strength in the four of them together. Still, he knew that his place was at his wife's side, and so he stayed. Besides, Kidwell's safety rested in hands far more capable than his. It was an act of faith every time she went out into a hazardous world alone, but then, they had all learned that there was good reason for faith, real faith. Still, it had been easier when the four of them stood together, and he would always value the memories formed during their journey through the backwoods to Thunder Lake where the people of the Taos Pueblo gave them haven at one of their most sacred sites.

He remembered clearly the fear when Kidwell's Navy contacts leaked a warning that they were all in danger. Kidwell and Anna for the message White Buffalo Calf Woman had given Kidwell about Desert Lightning, and Aisha and Greg for the message the spirits of Khadija and The Prophet had given Aisha about The Scimitar. The invasion code-named Desert Lightning aborted when all ordnance throughout the Middle East failed to fire and the terrorist attack code-named The Scimitar magically failed with an unexploded bomb. Those who fed off war and mayhem needed someone to blame for the failure, and Kidwell and Aisha were likely scapegoats. So, they'd headed for the high country of the Rocky Mountains of northeastern New Mexico, guided by Kidwell and Anna's knowledge of the backcountry and the continuing magic of spirit messages to Kidwell and Aisha.

Greg's thoughts wandered. He smiled softly as he remembered the lodge he and Aisha had shared beside Thunder Lake. Yes, it was there that the first segments of *The Book of Aisha* and *The Book of Kidwell* were written, and it was there that pilgrims came, guided by their own spirit voices, but what Greg remembered instead were those personal moments that were, perhaps, the happiest period of his entire life. He'd been spared most of the anxiety of Anna and Aisha's kidnapping, an unseen attacker having drugged him.

By the time he was fully awake, cared for by one of the pilgrims while he was unconscious, the battle was done, and his wife returned to him, unharmed except for a few bruises. The four allies then learned of the Dark One, once a man whom a dark spirit had deformed and possessed for over a century. Help came to Kidwell from her Spirit Guides, Martin Gonzales, the young Apache who had become Kidwell's right-hand man, and the pilgrims who rode with Kidwell and Martin. The Dark One and his followers, both in this world and the next, were defeated, and Anna and Aisha saved. Perhaps the whole world was saved.

No, not yet, Greg thought. The whole world was still endangered. He knew that, and he knew their work was not done. Sometimes he longed to see what that work would be, to know what was to come so that he could prepare, be ready for the task ahead. Never again did he want to sleep through the battle. It haunted him that he hadn't been there, despite assurances from Aisha and Kidwell that they understood. He did not know the attack was coming, and Kidwell assured him that he was the one drugged first because the kidnappers saw him as the greatest threat. He laughed at that thought.

"They didn't know Kidwell," he mumbled to himself.

Greg shook his head, bringing his mind back to the present. He glanced through emails, seeing none that required Aisha's personal attention. He was happy with the responses sent by the foundation's staff. This group consisted more of ministers and shaman than clerks, selected for their wisdom, good hearts, and intuitive connection to the spiritual. They did well. Greg turned his attention next to the stack of test papers from the undergraduate course on water science he taught, keeping his hand in academia.

⁂

As Greg worked, so did Aisha, but there was no quiet reflection in the intensity of her efforts. The vision she saw and the canvas before her consumed her fully, unaware of anything, including her own need for the food and drink Greg left for her. At one point, thirst finally scratched its way to awareness, and she downed the glass of ice water, never bothering to lay down her brush.

The scene coming to life under her hand was an alien world in ways beyond the bluish sun and two moons. It could have been a scene from an Asimov novel or something from a dream that danced on the edge of either nightmare or ecstasy, quite capable of going either direction. The world was a surprise, but the occupants gave life to a different reality. Their faces – whole bodies, actually – were a perfect balance of feline and human. Even in the stillness of a painting, one could feel the lithe grace of the two figures, one male and one female with fine fur-covered faces and hands visible outside the clothing. Obvious warriors, the hilt of a sword could be seen over the male's shoulder from where it was handily strapped to his back. A bow and quiver of arrows peeped over the female's shoulder, and they each had a deadly dirk sheathed at their wide, leather belts. They looked so alive that an observer would not be surprised to see them step from the painting and into the studio.

Aisha worked like a madwoman, not even stepping back from the painting until the last brushstroke completed the face of the green-eyed female. Dropping the brush into the jar to keep the acrylic paint moist until it could be washed away, Aisha sat, exhausted, in a paint-spotted chair she kept in her studio. For the first time, she noticed the plate of food Greg had left, and she consumed it in a greedy gobble. She looked at the painting, surprised at what she had created.

"Where did that come from?" Aisha asked herself. She didn't wonder for long. She drank the water from the melted ice in the glass, and rose to shuffle off to the bedroom. She needed a nap.

As she left the room, the faces of the feline pair turned, watching her leave. When she was gone, they looked at one another, smiling happily. They barely had time to return to their original positions, freezing all movement, as Greg entered the studio carrying two cups of coffee. Once he'd registered that his wife was no longer there, he set one cup on a table and then stood, mesmerized by the painting. It spoke well of his steady hand that he spilled only a small amount of coffee on the front of his shirt when the female feline winked at him.

Chapter Three

Homecoming

Kidwell couldn't hold back the tears as Martin pulled the Jeep around the last curve, and she could see her home. Home! She was finally home. She prayed it would be a very long time before she was called away again. Mainly, she longed to see Anna, and still felt a knot of disappointment from when she walked through the airport to find Martin Gonzales, her friend and assistant, waiting for her instead of Anna. She was glad to see Martin, hugging the young man like a long, lost friend, but it wasn't the same as her lover, her spouse greeting her. Martin knew Kidwell too well.

"She wanted to get everything ready for you at home," the young Apache said, answering Kidwell's unasked question.

Martin drove the Jeep Patriot during the long journey from Albuquerque to the remote compound where they all lived, nestled in the Rocky Mountains. Despite her exhaustion, Kidwell found herself babbling to Martin. Her rambling processed so much of her experiences in Mexico, and relieved her starvation for the communication with those whom she trusted and loved. Living in a remote village with little to no telephone service denied her that closeness. The convent had the only phone line, which was dead much of the time, and absolutely no Internet. She had once told Anna that nothing Kidwell did or saw seemed totally real until she'd shared it with Anna. For now, Martin was the short-term substitute. He listened with little comment, a smile on his face, pleased to have his friend and mentor safely home.

Occasionally, Kidwell was abruptly silent, mesmerized by the sight of her beloved New Mexico desert and, as they drove northeast, the Sangre de Cristo Mountains, part of the southern range of the great Rockies. In all honesty, there had been many moments when she had wondered if she would live to see it all again, something she did not intend to tell Anna.

Conversation totally ceased when they drove out of the "S" curves into the high valley where Kidwell could catch her first glimpse of the home she had shared with Anna for nearly ten years. Since returning from Thunder Lake, an office building with a small apartment for Martin had been added and the barn had been expanded, including an apartment for a groundskeeper and groom. Kidwell and Anna had been unable to keep up with their property and animals once the "prophet calling" invaded their lives. Before Kidwell left for the Yucatan, they had not yet hired anyone for that position, and Kidwell hoped Anna had found someone during her absence. She did not like to think she had imposed those additional duties on Anna and Martin while she was away.

"Welcome home," Martin said, as they pulled into the yard.

Kidwell used her shirtsleeve to wipe absently at the tears in her eyes. Martin stopped the Jeep directly beside the front porch where Anna stood, waiting. Kidwell was out the door and up the steps before Martin had time to kill the engine. He smiled at the sight of their reunion, putting the Jeep into gear and driving toward the garage, leaving the two women alone. He would carry Kidwell's pack and suitcase into the house through the kitchen entrance for he felt that this private reunion was particularly important. He felt the increasingly familiar cold chunk of dread in the pit of his stomach. *Kidwell's home*, he thought. *Everything will be fine now.*

For the longest time, Kidwell and Anna held each other and cried without moving from the front porch. This had been Kidwell's longest absence, especially without the possibility of daily communication. Each day, Kidwell wrote to Anna, and sent the multi-phase letter with the mail truck that visited the village once each week. There was always a letter from Anna waiting for her as well. Frequently, letters from Aisha or Martin or business correspondence from Admiral O'Hare waited as well. None had been enough. Kidwell had experienced the worst homesickness of her life.

Finally, Anna pushed away, holding Kidwell's face between her hands.

"You were away too long," Anna said with a Latina's passionate anger.

Kidwell laughed tearfully. "I'll say," she agreed.

Anna took Kidwell's hand and led her through the front door, through the house, and to the kitchen. Kidwell's pack and suitcase were by the back door, and Martin was already gone. Kidwell laughed in joy at what awaited her on the kitchen table – coconut cream pie.

"Anna, you made my favorite, but I usually make the pie. Where are your *empanadas*?" Kidwell asked.

"You've been in Mexico for two months," Anna responded. "I thought you'd be missing your pie, not *empanadas*."

Anna gathered two cups from the cabinet and poured fresh decaf coffee waiting in the coffee maker while Kidwell gathered plates and forks. Kidwell sliced the pie, putting a generous piece on each of two plates while Anna put cream and sugar in both coffees. As they both sat at the table, the weeks apart melted away. They laughed and talked, catching up on each other's lives. Kidwell made Anna laugh as she told of the village children's efforts to teach her Spanish and a smattering of the local indigenous language. Her first evening there, the children gathered around, fascinated with Kidwell's blue eyes, with one little girl crawling in her lap and asking frankly, "*¿Usted es un angel?*" Kidwell had been assuring the child she was no angel.

After a time, they placed the dirty dishes in the sink, and Anna took the suitcase and Kidwell the pack. They headed up the stairs to the room they'd shared for nearly ten years. Once there, Kidwell dropped the pack on the floor, and took the handle of the suitcase. Anna lay on the bed, watching Kidwell unpack, and they continued to talk. Kidwell told of the extra week that she'd had to spend in Mexico City, finding the right caretaker and scholar to entrust with the earthen jar given her by Tonantzin.

"Tonantzin?" Anna asked.

"Yes, the goddess who is also Our Lady of Guadalupe."

Anna sat upright on the bed. "You met Our Lady of Guadalupe?"

Kidwell paused in unloading the pack, placing mud-caked hiking pants in the hamper. She looked at her lover.

"Oh, honey, this story needs to be told all at one sitting with no distractions."

"What if I die of curiosity?"

Kidwell reached to squeeze Anna's hand. "Then I'll have to die of grief so we can be together, and I can tell you the story." They both laughed.

"I have something for you," Kidwell said as she opened the case. She took a cardboard tube from inside and opened it, carefully withdrawing a rolled canvas. It was a beautiful painting of Tonantzin in her feathered headdress and embroidered clothing. "She reminded me of you," Kidwell said.

Anna laughed. "A goddess reminded you of me? That's a stretch."

Kidwell looked at her partner with eyes so bright blue that the color was like a clear day, a sure sign Kidwell was deeply moved. "Not at all, my love," she responded.

Anna blushed but did not answer. She peered inside the open suitcase; there was a second item wrapped in tissue paper.

"What's that?" Anna asked.

"I got it from the same artists' market near the university. It called my name louder than any piece of art I've ever seen," Kidwell said. She unwrapped the paper from a piece of rough wood, the bark still around the edges. It was a first cut from a log with a mill saw having removed a protruding knot from a large log. Kidwell flipped the piece over, putting the bark-side to the back, and Anna gasped. The opposite side was a painting of a perfect eye, gloriously green with an elongated pupil like that of a cat.

"How magnificent," Anna said.

"Here's the real kicker," Kidwell responded, turning the painting to look at the rough side. "In ink, there's a symbol on the back that's just like the tattoo on Aisha's hand."

"That's amazing," Anna said.

Kidwell removed a photo of an old barn from the wall beside the bed and hung the "eye" in its place. "How's that?" she asked.

"Great, much better than the barn."

"Somehow, I feel this eye protects me," Kidwell said.

"*Querida*, you definitely need protection," Anna said, a hint of bitterness in her voice.

Kidwell looked at Anna quizzically for an instant and then returned to unpacking. "Sweetheart, it's wonderful to be home."

"There were times I despaired that you'd never return."

Kidwell pulled still clean underwear from the bag, and placed them in a drawer. "Surely you knew if there was the breath in my body that I'd be back to you," Kidwell said.

"Yes, I knew that," Anna answered, strain in her voice.

Kidwell stopped what she was doing and looked intently at her lover. "Anna, you know better than anyone that I'm called to do dangerous things, but I have protectors like no others."

"I know," Anna answered. "I also know that if they choose to take you from me, there is nothing I can do."

Kidwell shook her head. "Anna, that's true of

everyone."

Anna rose from the bed and walked determinedly to the master bathroom. "I'll run you a hot bath," she said. Kidwell knew then that the conversation was over, for now.

Despite the unpleasant twist to the conversation, Kidwell truly enjoyed the luxurious warmth of the bath. The week in Mexico City had been spent at a quality hotel, a room provided by one of Kidwell's many supporters in the network facilitated by the foundation. It had provided a buffer for her return to the comforts of home after weeks in a primitive hut in the Yucatan. Still, there was nothing better than home, that place where she could totally be herself. Anna stayed with her, and they spoke in soft voices of nothing and everything. It felt much like it had been during their first months together, totally absorbed in each other's company.

As Kidwell washed her hair, Anna left, returning to the bedroom. After Kidwell finished toweling and drying her hair, she put on the t-shirt and gym shorts that still hung on the back of the bathroom door from before she left for Mexico. She walked into the bedroom to find Anna in bed, waiting for her.

At that moment, nothing else mattered. Kidwell removed the shorts and t-shirt, dropping them to the floor, and crawled nude between the covers. What followed was an expression of love that words or actions, outside the bubble of intimacy, can never be fully duplicated. There, together in that moment, their souls intertwined as they had through a hundred lifetimes, without need for words or understanding of the current circumstances that affected their life together. There was nothing but pleasure and joy as intense as when they'd first found one another, only better because of their years of gaining appreciation and understanding of that which gave the other pleasure. They knew the little unexpected sites on the skin's surface where nerves bundled to provide waves of pleasure throughout the body. They knew exactly what the other liked. It was sex with a level of tenderness possible only when physical pleasure married deep love. There was no hurry to what they shared. Outside, the day lengthened into twilight until finally they lay together, sated and content.

Anna nestled her face comfortably into the nap of Kidwell's neck, whispering softly.

"Promise you'll never leave me again."

Kidwell felt a tension replace the languid warmth. At first, she answered only with silence. She felt Anna tense as well, although neither of them changed position.

"Darling, you know that's a promise I cannot make," Kidwell answered.

Anna raised herself onto one elbow, looking at her lover. "Then promise you will always come back to me."

Kidwell looked at Anna, stunned. "Sweetheart, why do you ask impossible promises? I can promise that you are in my heart no matter where I must go, and if the spirits allow, I will always come back to you."

Anna sat on the edge of the bed, speaking over her shoulder. "When you retired from the Navy, we bought this place so that we could live a quiet life together."

"I did not plan this, Anna."

Anna rose abruptly and put on sweatpants and a shirt. "It's getting late. We need to fix dinner."

Kidwell watched as Anna left the room and went down the stairs. The joy of homecoming was suddenly tainted, like sawdust in honey. Kidwell had no idea what had happened or what to do about it. She comforted herself with the memory that this was not the first fight she'd had with her fiery Latina. *This would pass*, she thought, before rising from the bed and dressing to go down and help prepare a meal.

Chapter Four

The Smell of Darkness

Kidwell's butt truly felt that it had come home. She nestled into the slightly ragged office chair that she'd used for nearly fifteen years, automatically positioning it so that she wasn't lopsided, avoiding the spot where the chair was slightly sprung. For eight years, Anna had threatened to throw away the chair, and Kidwell had promised that as soon as it broke beyond usability, it would go into the trash. Somehow, the battle-scarred chair always seemed to make it through one more year.

The stack of papers on her desk wasn't nearly as bad as it could have been. She was grateful for those who had stepped into her life to relieve her of the burden of daily business after she'd been called to life as a prophet, a role in which she still felt amazingly uncomfortable and inadequate. Still, she had learned long ago that if she was given a job, she did it. If her best wasn't good enough, well, that was all she had to offer. Martin, Admiral O'Hare, Greg, Anna, and a host of others made it possible for her to continue her calling without having to sacrifice her home and whatever sense of normalcy was still possible for Kidwell. She did have to give up some things. One of the most painful was the local fire department. Her bunkers for structure fires as well as her wild-land gear still hung from hooks in the mudroom at the back of the house, and when she didn't have other obligations, she left the radio on, listening for a page. It was rare that she was free to respond as a plain old volunteer firefighter. Not often was she free from awaiting a phone call or a visit or else being called into the woods by a whisper from White Buffalo Calf Woman. Everything else came to a halt when such a call came. It was the mystical lessons and messages upon which Kidwell's life now revolved. In many ways, that life had become more real to her than that of daily living. Kidwell's surreal existence had become normal for her.

Kidwell left Anna still sleeping. The tension between them the night before had evaporated by the time they finished preparing a meal of broiled fish, butter and parsley potatoes, and fresh salad with Anna's special chipotle/honey dressing. They laughed together as they washed the dishes, Anna bringing Kidwell up-to-date on the running plot of the sci-fi television show they both enjoyed. Both slept better than they had in weeks, safely curled in each other's arms. The cat, Milagra, spent the entire night sleeping on or near Kidwell, putting both women to sleep with the sound of her purrs.

When morning came, Kidwell awoke excited, ready to step back into her normal life. Sleepy-eyed, Kidwell first started for the mudroom, preparing to put on boots and head out to feed the horses. Then she remembered Anna telling her that she had hired a caretaker who now ensured the animals were fed and the grounds kept in order. Although she knew it was necessary, Kidwell felt a momentary sadness at the loss of that daily routine. She promised herself that the day would include a ride on her aging Appaloosa.

Sometime soon, she would need to find a new horse and give her loyal steed a well-deserved retirement, but not yet. She still had some good days ahead with him. She intended for this day to be one of them, but first, there was business awaiting her.

Martin and Admiral O'Hare did their best to shoulder the burden of daily business for Kidwell and Anna. Regular bills were on an automatic withdrawal from bank accounts, and a contract accountant kept up the books with bi-monthly summaries given to Martin, Kidwell, and Anna. Copies of those summaries were included in Kidwell's inbox. She glanced through, assuring herself that there were sufficient funds to cover all personal needs. There was a new line item for a property caretaker, and Kidwell was surprised to see that the individual was paid more than Martin. She'd have to ask Anna why. There were only three letters in the stack, all of them from people who had some sort of personal tie to Kidwell. She would answer later. The most important piece was the newest additions to *The Book of Kidwell* and *The Book of Aisha*. They still worked with the same publisher, a man who had been "called" to make the books public, and they were still printed as new sections and distributed to be added to binders in the hands of millions of readers worldwide. Although Kidwell and Aisha both submitted drafts for new sections to the publisher, he would not release anything without final approval from the two women. Kidwell would make reading those additions a top priority. She knew that those books made the spiritual gifts she received applicable to a far wider audience. Also, she looked forward to reading Aisha's piece. That always brought her joy and new insights. Kidwell's latest addition – the story of her encounters in the Yucatan – was still a hand-written draft. There had been no computer or even a typewriter for her to use. She would copy the piece and send the copy to the publisher. It was not the first time they'd dealt with this issue.

Kidwell heard the backdoor open and shortly thereafter, Martin stuck his head around the door to her office.

"You had breakfast?" he asked.

"Nope," Kidwell answered. "But I made fresh coffee."

"Saw it. Want to take a break and have breakfast with me?"

"Sure," Kidwell said. "You know Anna, she likes her beauty sleep."

It felt great to step back into an old routine. She and Martin usually had breakfast together. Martin fried bacon while Kidwell made scrambled eggs topped with salsa and cheese. They settled for toast since Kidwell had forgotten to start fresh biscuits. Frequently, breakfast for the two was just biscuits and a fruit mix, but today was special. Kidwell was home.

Martin started catching Kidwell up on business. He told her about the pilgrims who had visited in her absence and some of the requests they'd received for Kidwell to speak to different groups. She rarely accepted unless she felt "called." Sometimes there were offers of many thousands of dollars to speak at national conventions, but Kidwell had yet to accept such an offer. Perhaps it was an innate prejudice within her, but she felt that the affluent and successful were rarely ready to hear the messages she was given.

Admiral O'Hare had a plan to address the growing number of requests received from those who wanted some sort of structure and guidance. Both Kidwell and Aisha were adamant that no new "religion" be formed based on the lessons they'd been given. Kidwell especially emphasized that spiritual growth was an individual journey, not an exodus of the masses. In response, O'Hare formed a plan for spiritual development centers, places where people with a vision could apply to use the facility for meditation rooms, drum circles, lecture halls – efforts to nurture seekers on their own journey. There were now two in operation, one in Santa Fe and another in upstate New York. Kidwell and Aisha had participated closely in selecting directors for those facilities, with each prophet seeking guidance from spirit guides as well. In each case, both women and O'Hare felt that the right person had been chosen for the job, and Kidwell rarely thought about it again. The delegation system worked. When the requests came for group support, they were simply referred to the Centers.

Throughout preparation and consumption of the meal, Kidwell and Martin spoke with the ease of a long and deep friendship. Kidwell felt as though Martin was as close to a son as anyone she would ever know, and he returned her depth of love and respect. They talked business with ease, and Kidwell was able to give Martin the abbreviated version of her spiritual experiences in Mexico, for he knew well what that was like for her, needing no explanation or background.

As they finished breakfast, Martin rose to pour them each a final cup of coffee. Kidwell watched as his demeanor changed. His hands moved nervously, and he cleared his throat as though what he needed to say would not exit of its own free will. He sat back down at the table and stirred his cup far longer than needed to mingle coffee, sugar, and milk.

"What's up, bud?" Kidwell asked.

Martin took a deep breath. "Kid, some things happened while you were gone. I'm worried."

"What happened?" Kidwell asked, a knot of concern crowding in with the eggs in her stomach.

"Anna…while you were gone…" Martin started.

The kitchen door opened abruptly. A strange woman stepped inside. She was thin with artificially red hair – not unattractive, but something about her made the hairs stand up on the back of Kidwell's neck. Her soul recognized the woman, an old enemy from past lives. The woman wore boots, jeans, and a faded denim shirt.

"Hello, who are you?" Kidwell demanded.

"Kidwell, this is Celia Martinez, the caretaker Anna hired while you were gone," Martin said. He looked deep into Kidwell's gaze, and Kidwell knew she had just met the source of Martin's concern.

Kidwell stood and faced the woman. Neither offered a hand to the other.

"I'm here to report to Anna," Celia said.

"She's sleeping late this morning," Kidwell answered.

Celia glanced at the clock over the kitchen cabinet. "It's nearly ten. She'll want me to wake her."

"No, she won't," Kidwell answered.

Celia glared at Kidwell. "I guess you're Kidwell."

"You guess right, but, for now, I would prefer you call me Ms. Brown."

Martin rose, standing a head taller than either woman. Celia looked between the two, and her attitude changed. For a second, a glare of hatred flickered toward Martin.

"Welcome back," Celia said. The words were kind, but there was a hint of sarcasm in her voice. "I guess I better get back to the barn."

"Yes, that's a good idea," Kidwell said. "Oh, and Miss Martinez…"

"Yes?"

"Next time, knock."

To her credit, Celia attempted a smile, but it looked more like a sneer. "Yes, ma'am." She left, closing the door a little too sharply behind her.

"What the hell?" Kidwell said.

"Yep, that's what I wanted to tell you," Martin responded.

"How long's she been here?" Kidwell asked.

"About six weeks." They both returned to the table, sitting to finish their coffee. "She showed up one evening when everything was going wrong. The bay mare had cut herself on the fence, and we had a group of pilgrims camping next to the house, not the best bunch. A pot of beans burned on the stove in the house while we were juggling everything else. We turned off the pot and had to open all the windows to clear out the smoke. Anna was dealing with the mare and the vet, and I was trying to get the pilgrims to move down to the campground by the river. Celia just showed up and started feeding horses and helping the vet. She glared once at the pilgrims, and they decided to move. Even I was glad to see her that evening, but…"

"But what?"

"I swear, somehow I think Celia made it all happen, created a big drama so we'd welcome her here."

Kidwell raised her nose to the air and closed her eyes, sniffing deeply. "Smell it?"

"Sometimes I do," Martin answered. "Like the Dark One, the one who planned the kidnapping of Anna and Aisha."

"The smell of evil," Kidwell said.

"Yeah," Martin responded. "What are we going to do?"

"Anna smell it?"

Martin's lips tightened into a thin line. "No, Celia's all sugar and sweet when she's around Anna."

Kidwell felt a cold knot of fear, unlike any she'd ever known. She'd rather have a gun in her face than this wave of uncertainty.

"I don't know, Martin. I don't know what to do, but, when the time is right, we'll do it," Kidwell said.

"Thank God you're home," Martin said.

They both jumped as the phone rang. Kidwell walked to the cordless phone hanging by the back door.

"Hello," she answered. There was a pause. "Admiral! So good to hear from you." Pause. "Yeah, I can meet you on Skype. I'll head for the computer now. Talk with you in a few."

Kidwell hung up and turned to Martin. "We'll talk later."

"Sure, Kid, but I'm just glad I'm not trying to deal with this alone anymore."

"I thank God you were here while I was gone," Kidwell responded.

Admiral O'Hare had a lot to discuss. It would be over an hour before Kidwell turned off the computer and went looking for Anna. When she went upstairs, the bed was empty and made up. Anna was gone, and the cold knot of fear in Kidwell's stomach grew exponentially.

They'd ridden a familiar route, down the county road by the house and up a logging road to the ridgeline trail. It had become a daily habit for Anna and Celia to take two of the five horses on a ride for an hour or two each morning. Since they'd begun that routine, all the horses seemed happier and healthier, except Kidwell's Appaloosa. He was running loose in the pasture by the river, his mane full of burrs. Every time Celia came close to him, the gelding bared his teeth and, at times, even tried to paw her.

"Sometimes horses get cranky when they get old," Celia explained.

"And he loves Kidwell more than anyone," Anna added. Anna approached the gelding, and he settled down immediately. He gently nestled his face against her chest. "I know, Smokey," she whispered. "I miss her too."

In the end, they'd decided to turn the Appaloosa out to pasture while Kidwell was away. Anna did not have the time to care for him, and he was obviously unwilling to let Celia be his handler. Anna was surprised, for she saw a gentle tenderness in Celia as she groomed and fed the horses, a gentleness she rarely saw in Celia during her interactions with other people. That gentle hand with horses had been the primary reason Anna ignored Martin when he awkwardly expressed discomfort with the new groundskeeper. Besides, Celia listened to Anna and was the only person with whom Anna felt free to express her feelings of being neglected since Kidwell became a worldwide celebrity.

At first, Anna felt badly at Smokey's banishment from the barn, but the aging horse grew fat on the abundant grass. Celia alternated which horse pastured with Smokey. Anna would watch from the kitchen window as the horses played as though they were once again young foals. Smokey enjoyed the easy freedom.

When Anna came downstairs, ready for the morning ride, she found Kidwell at her desk, deep in a teleconferenced conversation with Admiral O'Hare. Kidwell didn't even notice Anna standing in the doorway. Anna swallowed the bitterness of disappointment, having dreamed for weeks of Kidwell once again riding by her side. There had been so much happiness in their years together, but none compared to the time they'd spent riding side-by-side, exiled to the hidden valley of Thunder Lake.

Anna rode her red sorrel up to the hitching post and dismounted. Celia stopped the bay mare at the far end of the hitching post and stepped to the ground. They each unsaddled their horses, carrying saddles and saddle pads to the tack-room, retrieving curry combs and brushes to brush away the sweat of exertion from the horses' backs and, today, even their chests and bellies. The logging road was steep, causing the mounts to work a little harder. Anna paused in her brushing to look toward the house, wondering if Kidwell was still working.

"I can't believe she neglected you this morning," Celia said, her mouth set in a hard line. "Not on her first day back."

"You don't understand," Anna responded.

"Do you?" Celia demanded.

Anna brushed harder, making the sorrel shy slightly away. "No, not really," she answered, "But I don't have the experiences or the burdens Kidwell faces."

Celia gave a derisive laugh. "What could be so important that someone would neglect the one they love?"

Anna said nothing. Instead, she untied her gelding from the rail, and walked him toward the corral, hoping Celia did not see the glint of tears in her eyes. It was not the first time Anna had this conversation or one like it with Celia. She'd grown weary of defending Kidwell, and, increasingly, she heard more sense in Celia's arguments than she wanted to admit.

The sound of the screen door swinging closed carried across the yard. Anna looked up to see Kidwell walking toward her. She felt her breath quicken, somehow reminiscent of the first time she'd spotted Kidwell across the room at a community meeting.

"Did you have a good ride?" Kidwell asked. She walked close to Anna and brushed a strand of hair out of her lover's eyes.

"Yes," Anna answered, feeling an unexpected and confusing cocktail of emotion including joy and anger. She continued leading her sorrel toward the corral, and Kidwell walked beside her.

"I'm sorry I wasn't with you. I've missed our rides. Sometimes, in the hut in Mexico, I would put myself asleep remembering riding side-by-side with you."

Anna was so engorged with emotion that confusion enveloped her. She felt an intense need for time and space to sort out her emotions. Once she'd removed the halter from the gelding, he stood waiting for her to scratch his ears and face as she always did, but instead, she gathered up the halter and headed for the tack-room.

"I need to start lunch," she said as she walked

away. She stopped after a few steps and turned to face Kidwell. "I'm angry, Kid."

"I know," Kidwell answered with a light of hurt in her eyes. "I can see that. Anna, I love you, and I do not wish to spend time away from you, from our life together."

A single tear trickled down Anna's cheek. "Couldn't Admiral O'Hare have waited?" Anna demanded.

"Yes, he could have. If I'd known you wanted to ride with me, I would have ended the call," Kidwell responded.

"But you didn't."

"What? End the call or know you wanted to ride?"

Anna threw her hands into the air in a wild gesture. She mumbled in Spanish as she stomped toward the tack-room to leave the halter, continuing the angry stomp as she walked toward the house.

Kidwell smiled in secret relief as she watched. She recognized the anger of her passionate Latina, and she remembered wonderful reconciliations from the past. Perhaps Martin was right; all would be well now that Kidwell was home again.

Kidwell heard someone clear their throat behind her. She turned to see Celia leading the bay mare.

"Excuse me," Celia said with anything but politeness in the tone of her voice.

Kidwell glanced to the left and right. There was plenty of room for Celia and the horse to pass.

"No," Kidwell answered.

The flash of surprise in Celia's eyes was gratifying to Kidwell. "I thought you were some great, gentle healer," Celia said, sarcasm apparent in every word.

"And a warrior," Kidwell answered.

For a moment, there was fear mixed with the surprise in Celia's eyes. The groundskeeper's gaze dropped to the ground, and she led the horse in an arch around where Kidwell stood.

"Celia," Kidwell called.

The woman stopped and looked back, defiant. "Yes?"

"Don't get too comfortable. Anna and I need to review and discuss the applications for groundskeeper."

Celia stood with her mouth open. This was not what she expected.

Kidwell walked toward the tack-room.

"What are you doing?" Celia demanded.

"Getting a halter for Smokey. He needs to be groomed," Kidwell answered.

"Don't mess up my tack-room," Celia said.

Kidwell laughed and turned to face her opponent. "Whose tack-room?"

Celia turned on her heel and continued toward the corral. This had not been what she expected. All her life she'd lived in a Christian family. People rarely pushed back. They had always tried to make her happy, appease her. She didn't know what to do.

Kidwell watched the other woman walk away. Suddenly she wasn't so certain that Martin was correct. Maybe her return from Mexico wouldn't set things right as easily as he hoped.

⁂

Celia had no clue who or what hovered above her

as she watched from the window of her apartment over the barn. Martin would have smelled him, as would Kidwell, perhaps even Anna if she had been this close. The foul creature hung close, just as he'd done since Celia was a child, petulant and angry when she didn't get her way. Over the years, the evil being had created a direct link between himself and the increasingly black heart of the angry woman. He'd fed her sense of entitlement, a skewed view of what was fair and what was unfair. In time, Celia grew to define right as getting what she wanted and wrong as anything that stood in her way. Soon he would have her, own her very being and body as if it were his own and the soul that was Celia would be relegated to some dark corner of her being with little consciousness and no control. The gift, if one wanted to call it that, of near immortality would come with the full possession. The demon had known of some to possess the same body for well over a century, and he looked forward to the power he would have when he could walk among humanity as one of their own. He was close, so very close, although he flashed in anger at Celia's love of horses. The demon had little power over the woman when in the presence of such magical beasts. Only the influence he planted in her mind – the hate, the entitlement, the deceptions – held sway when he could not be near her. It had worked in his favor in this case. Celia's love of horses, who she was when in their presence, had enabled Celia to seduce her way into the home of the prophet whom he hated, whom all his kind hated.

Celia seethed with anger as she watched Martin go into the main house through the kitchen door. Some of the anger was her own, but the demon who was her unseen companion fed and nurtured most of the anger. In the weeks while Kidwell was gone, Celia had usurped his position as a daily lunch visitor. At first, the three of them, Anna, Martin, and Celia, had all gathered in the kitchen for the mid-day meal, but the tension had increased with Celia's veiled criticism of the absent prophet. She had been so subtle that Anna barely noticed, but Martin did. In less than two weeks, he'd just stopped coming for lunch. With his absence, Celia gradually increased her implications and innuendos, and she could see the doubts, the pain she helped instill in Anna.

Now, with Kidwell home, Martin was back in his place at the kitchen table. Celia knew she could go down, invite herself to the meal, but she still stung from the conversation with Kidwell. The methods she'd used all her life would not work with this woman. She'd underestimated the prophet. New tactics would be required. As she continued to stare out the window, there was a whisper to her very soul from a being whose presence had been a long-time companion of which she'd never been aware. An evil smile appeared on her lips. A plan was taking shape.

Chapter Five

Safety for Monsters

Despondence marked his mood as Roberto read the report before him. Written in perfect English by a fellow speaker of his native Spanish tongue, it told a tale that was not what he hoped to see. Kidwell Brown had failed. During most of his six years as an assistant prosecutor for the UN's International Court of Justice, Roberto had prayed to bring to justice the drug lord preying upon his own Mayan people. Although Roberto was Costa Rican by birth, in many ways his deepest loyalties were to the Maya, not the descendants of *Hispaña*. The authorities of Mexico were more than willing to extradite the *pendejo* to The Hague for trial and punishment, and Roberto had traveled to Mexico City on three occasions to plan for just such a contingency. The reality was that bringing the man to justice would trigger a bloody war more horrific than the violations currently committed by the monster. Roberto knew it, the Mexican *federales* knew it, and the despicable drug lord knew it.

There had been some success in capturing and trying the drug lord's lieutenants, for, occasionally, they had to travel outside the well-armed enclave that protected the heart of the drug lord's operations. Intel occasionally located a lieutenant outside of the lair, and even though arrests had included some fatal battles, at least a dent was made in the power of the monster. The drug lord never left. All the fineries of life, including beautiful sex slaves, were imported to him, but the drug lord never left the safety of his fortress.

The same Mother Superior who had requested Kidwell's help in a bid for peace had been a long-time informant to the ICJ. The courageous and dedicated nun had obtained many of the photos and testimonies in the file Roberto now reviewed. He feared for her life and for the lives of those who helped her.

Roberto removed his glasses, rubbed at his tired eyes, and rose from his desk chair. He looked out the window to the busy street below. He had grown to love Holland and was now accustomed to the curious looks caused by his dark complexion and the facial features he'd inherited from both his Mayan mother and *mestizaje* – mixed-blood – father. It was uncommon for a Mayan to walk the streets of The Hague. At least in the neighborhood where he lived, people no longer stared, and his Dutch was now proficient, making him able to live among his neighbors as one of them. Still, he would never be able to acclimatize to the damp cold that crept into the very core of his Mayan bones. Vacations were spent at home, basking in the sun on the beach or walking jungle trails.

Over time, Holland had grown to feel like home. Despite the cold, he would miss it when the time came for Roberto to leave his post. At least once each year, he took the train to Amsterdam and visited the Anne Frank Museum. It reminded him why he did what he did as an officer of the ICJ, also known as the World Court. The corruption at the heart of the Nazi movement always had the threat of germination in another place, among other people. Ideally, the World

Court helped prevent such crimes against humanity – when it could. Frequently, it could not, for within the borders of any nation, political and physical realities limited the World Court. Many nights Roberto lay awake, thinking of the massive killings in the Congo, the matrix of trafficking in sex slaves throughout much of the world. Frequently, the heart of evil could be traced to a small group or even a single individual. He wished, prayed even, that he could do more to protect the people of the world and even the Earth itself. The reality was that, all too often, there was safety for monsters who built a wall of protection around themselves, and a prison around those they victimized. Although it broke his heart, Roberto had learned to live with knowing what he could address and what he could not. It was part of the price of the job.

Roberto opened the file again, and looked at the latest photo sent by the Mother Superior. The man's face was gone, destroyed by a high caliber pistol. He had been one of the field workers kidnapped and forced into slavery by the drug lord. When the man tried to escape, he had been hunted like a wild beast and left to rot in the jungle. Roberto looked long and hard at the picture. It could have easily been his uncle – the same muscled body of a hard-working Mayan.

"I would avenge you, if I could," Roberto said to the photo.

When Roberto heard that the famous Kidwell Brown had agreed to try to negotiate a peace, Roberto had been hopeful. There were stories of other miracles. If the drug lord changed his ways, Roberto could forget the desire for vengeance. He just prayed that the killing, the slavery, the starvation of his people would stop.

"If only there was a way," he whispered. "If only

there was a way."

❧ ❧ ❧ ❧

Smokey pranced like a colt when Kidwell climbed into the saddle; Martin already mounted on his paint mare, patiently waiting. It had taken time to curry comb the burrs from Smokey's mane and tail. It was a good ride, although Kidwell still tasted a hint of bitter disappointment that it was Martin, not Anna at her side. They had ridden along the river, stopping once to pick and eat apples from one of the wild trees near a home-site that had been abandoned for eighty years. Smokey had grabbed an apple for himself from one of the lower branches. Despite his years, the horse had been a handful during the ride, expressing his displeasure at Kidwell's long absence. Horses and riders were both pleasantly tired as they returned to the barn.

Kidwell and Martin dismounted, tying the reins to the hitching post near the tack-room. Kidwell paused after dropping her saddle so that it stood on horn and swells. She held a soft brush in her hand, preparing to brush the sweat from Smokey's back where the saddle had rested.

"Do you feel it?" Kidwell asked.

Martin stopped grooming his own horse. "The darkness?"

"Yes."

"Of course."

"Can't Anna feel it?"

Martin returned to brushing. "It's like a skunk under the house. After a while, you just don't smell it."

Kidwell's brushing became harder, causing

Smokey to step away. She forced herself to become gentler. "How could Anna let this happen?"

Martin stepped around both horses and looked at Kidwell eye-to-eye. "Anna bears a burden you cannot know, Kid. You face the battles, but she must wait, not knowing, wondering. It is lonely for her, and I think she fears she does not have the strength to be your mate."

Kidwell leaned against Smokey, tears stinging her eyes. She breathed deeply, comforted by the smell of horse.

"She must hate me for how I've changed our lives."

"Sometimes, maybe," Martin answered. "But it's not hate. It's fear."

Kidwell untied the reins from the post and led Smokey toward the corral. "It breaks my heart to cause Anna fear, but I cannot change what I am called to do." As she walked, Kidwell looked toward the window of the apartment above the barn. She saw the slight flicker of a curtain and knew she was being watched.

"Can she be saved?" Kidwell asked.

"Anna? Of course," Martin answered.

"Not Anna. Celia," Kidwell responded.

Martin looked up to the window as well. "I don't know, Kid. Frankly, I'm not sure I would be willing to try."

Chapter Six

Quests

It was now habit for Greg – the preparing of dinner and using a tray to carry the meal to Aisha's studio. At first, it had been rather fun watching the frenzied work of his talented wife. After nearly a month of obsessive work, he was far more worried than entertained.

Greg flipped the second omelet from the pan to plate, taking time to cut the toast into triangles and placing a dish of his wife's favorite jam on the tray. He poured glasses of the fruit juice mixture she liked, the taste of which almost always triggered a re-telling of Aisha's first visit with Kadijah and the Prophet Mohammed when her astral body had rested at an oasis, sharing figs and fruit juice with her spirit guides. It was the start of her mission as a prophet, a time she remembered with great joy and fear.

With the meal neatly arranged on a tray, Greg left the kitchen and walked toward Aisha's studio, moving slowly so as not to spill juice from the glasses. He entered a room so filled with color and exotic shapes that it was an assault on the senses. At least fifty large canvases leaned against the walls, three or four deep in some places. The work was magical, depicting no land or being Greg had ever seen before, at least not in the flesh. Some were mythological creatures he recognized – fairies, elves, dwarves, dragons, unicorns, angels, even grey aliens – while others were completely new to him. He was especially drawn to the first painting Aisha had created when the obsession began. It depicted a humanoid, feline couple – both dressed as warriors with swords, bucklers, bows and arrows – standing before a range of mountains, the vegetation surrounding them unique to their world with two moons seen in the deep blue daylight sky. The beauty of the beings and the land where they lived affected Greg oddly, almost bringing him to tears on multiple occasions. Twice he had stared at the painting for so long that his mind played tricks on him, convincing him he'd seen the twitch of a whisker or the flicker of an ear.

For nearly a month, Aisha had been driven to paint the visions that came to her almost non-stop. She slept soundly every night after dropping into bed in sheer exhaustion, but dreams of the sights and beings she would paint during the daylight hours filled her nights. Sometimes, Greg awakened in the night to hear his wife talking softly in her sleep. The sleep talking was not a major surprise, but the fact that it was in no human language he recognized came as a shock. Still, Greg learned long before to accept the magic as it came and adapt as best he could. Once he had worked through the macho stereotypes of his culture, he willingly accepted the role of consort to the prophet. Aisha bore a heavy burden, and she needed him. Greg decided that no man could have any greater calling.

Greg set the tray on the coffee table in front of the worn and paint smeared love seat that was part of Aisha's studio. It was where she sometimes rested, looking at her work from a distance, gaining perspective. Greg had timed the meal strategically, having learned over the past month to time preparation based on Aisha being near the completion of a painting. If it was six in the evening or nine, it didn't matter. She would not eat while the obsession consumed her. Greg watched his wife work, his heart feeling a twinge of fear as he saw how thin she'd become, with a slight stoop to her tired shoulders. There were moments when he wanted to hold her so tight she couldn't paint and demand that she rest, but he knew the effort would be futile. He could not stop the flow of paintings any more than he could will a river to pause in its path to the sea.

It only took a few minutes for Aisha to put the final touches on the highlights to the scales of a fearsome looking reptilian whose face and shoulders filled almost the entire canvas, leaving little room to show the world in which he lived. The fearsome stare of the being bore into Greg, causing a chill to give him a brief shiver. It was not his favorite of Aisha's paintings.

Greg had timed the meal well. The eggs were still warm as Aisha placed the brush in a jar to clean and turned to her husband. In a moment, Greg saw the shine of her obsession fade from her eyes, and he knew that her focus was entirely upon him. Her gaze softened, and she sat beside him, placing her hand over his.

"Of all the gifts I have been given, you are the most precious," she said, gently stroking his cheek.

"The feeling's mutual," he answered.

Aisha laughed with a hint of bitterness. "How can you say that after this past month?"

It was Greg's turn to laugh, *sans* bitterness. "I feel like Michelangelo's assistant must have felt as the master painted the Sistine Chapel. Maybe all I do is bring food and drink and buy the paint you need to do your work, but I am a small part of something great, doing it all for someone who means the world to me. If that's not a gift, what is?"

They kissed. Aisha was too exhausted for passion, but the kiss had great depth. Their love went far beyond the physical, the sexual. That kiss was a symbolic embrace of two souls – the type of kiss to which the couple had been long accustomed.

Hunger trumped affection in a short time, and Aisha turned her attention to the meal Greg had prepared. Greg was only half-finished with his plate of omelet, toast, and mixed fruit as Aisha finished chewing the last bite of her now empty plate. As she downed her glass of juice, the taste brought tears to her eyes, reminding her, as always, of her first meeting with her spirit mother, Kadijah. Kadijah had not visited Aisha even in her dreams for many weeks. Aisha missed her primary guide desperately and had moments of extreme self-doubt, concerned that the obsession that now drove her may not be rooted in the greater good. Her heart told her "yes, this is something you must do," but she would feel so much more confident with a simple nod of encouragement from Kadijah.

Aisha sighed and laid her head on the back of the loveseat as Greg finished his meal. As soon as he was done, he put his arm around her, and she rested her head on his shoulder. Within moments, she was breathing the soft, steady rhythm of deep sleep, and Greg settled comfortably in the couch, not wanting to disturb her. Without intending to do so, he soon slept as well, his soft snores making a duet with his wife's deep breaths.

There was a chill in the air, seeming to exude from the stone wall Greg now stood beside. He was surprised at the sensation for he was aware he was dreaming. He was perplexed, trying to remember if he'd ever before felt cold in a dream. The sound of laughter brought him back to the dream surroundings, and he looked down the hallway constructed of stone on the walls and a high ceiling with a heavy, wooden floor beneath. Tapestries hung at regular intervals, and as Greg stepped beside the nearest one, he felt a decrease in the chill. He smiled, amused at his revelation. So that's why they had so many tapestries, he thought. He heard the laughter again and realized the sound came from an open doorway at the end of the hallway. Greg walked in that direction, curious who was laughing in his dream.

He entered a huge room with a pair of thrones along one wall. Two men sat in adjacent chairs at a huge table in the center of the room. Each man was dressed in tunics, trousers, and tall boots with an overlay adorned in the image of a dragon covering most of their tunics. One man wore a thin ring of steel on his head, which Greg supposed was an "everyday" crown. This man laughed as he held cards before him, a pegged board on the table beside him. If Greg had any doubt who the man was, it certainly disappeared as Greg observed the table at which the two men sat. Surprise, surprise! It was round.

The man laughed again as he adjusted the pegs on the board. "Tough luck, Lance. I'm glad you're not nearly as good at cribbage as you are with a sword."

The now named Lance frowned good-naturedly.

"I just need practice, my Lord."

"Practice." The king laughed again. "After all these centuries, I'm not sure if you're just an inherently bad cribbage player or just smart enough to let the king win."

It was Lance's turn to laugh. "Care to take that theory with sword and shield out to the practice field?"

The king rubbed his left arm. "I still have the bruises from yesterday. It's settled, then. You're awful at cribbage." The king turned to face Greg. "So, you've finally arrived."

Greg started in surprise. He had assumed he was just an observer in this dream.

"Yes, I suppose I have," Greg answered. He looked at the king, confused. "Should I bow or something?"

"Good God, no," Arthur answered. "I'm just a warrior and a guardian, same as you. Different times and different ways required that entire royalty clap trap." The king gathered the deck of cards, preparing to shuffle. "Do you play cribbage?"

"No, I never learned," Greg answered.

"Too bad. Gwen's away in another world, and I'm crying for a good game."

"I'm sorry, my Lord. I just don't have the heart for this game," Lance answered.

"I know, old friend. Thank you for indulging me so while we waited for Greg to arrive."

"It was a pleasure," Lance said.

Arthur chucked his friend on the arm. "No, it wasn't, you benevolent liar you. Makes your patience all the more valued."

"No, it wasn't," Lance answered. "Will you need me further, sire?"

"Not for now. Go, go! I'm sure there's a hunt or

a joust or a tankard of ale in need of your attention."

Lance smiled and bowed his head slightly before rising quickly and striding out the door. Arthur motioned for Greg to take Lancelot's now empty chair.

"Do you know why you're here?" the king asked.

"Not a clue."

"We're the same, you and I," Arthur said. "We have a mission to protect and nurture those who make the magic. History named me as a great leader, but in reality, I was only a protector. What's that over-simplified phrase the books have given me – Might for Right?"

"I don't understand," Greg responded.

"People thought it was all about the power of a king, but it was about a king protecting an ideal, that honor, truth, and dignity should rule, not the man with the largest army or the champion who bests others with the sword. The real hero was honor, truth, and dignity, not me or Lancelot." A look of pain washed across Arthur's face. "I think that's why it failed in the end, because I allowed it to be about us – the king, the queen, and the man who was my champion. We were human and unable to live the ideal of honor, truth, and dignity."

"Arthur, your ideal lived. There are still those who strive to live by the code of honor you espoused." Greg paused, thinking deeply. "I'm one of them."

"I know," Arthur said. "Why else do you think you were chosen?"

"Chosen? For what?"

"To protect the prophets. Aisha and Kidwell may be the messengers, but you must help save them from those who would silence their message."

Greg laughed with a hint of bitterness. He still

remembered with great pain that he had been so easily drugged, totally unaware of the presence of an enemy, when Aisha and Anna had been kidnapped. While he was unconscious, Kidwell led their rescuers.

"Some protector I am," Greg said. "I've already failed once."

Arthur laughed. "No, my friend. Even the greatest warrior can be caught off guard, especially when they feel safe within their own battlements during times of peace. Besides, it was not yet your time to step into your role as protector."

"Is it now?"

"Soon," Arthur responded. "That's why you're here, for me to inform you that your teachers are coming soon. Be ready for them, accept them."

"Who are they?"

"You will know them when the time comes. You must be trained in the way of the warrior. In time, that will prove critical."

Greg sighed. "I hope I'm man enough for the job."

Arthur grasped Greg by the wrist. "My friend, if you had no doubts about your strength and wisdom, it would be positive proof that you had neither." The king started to gather up cards and cribbage board. "As much as I've enjoyed this, I'm afraid it is time for you to go."

"Thank you," Greg said. As he rose from the chair, he glanced at the image on the king's tunic. "Arthur, I've often wondered, why a dragon?"

Arthur looked down at a tapestry on the wall that displayed the same image as that over his tunic. "As a living man, I only knew that I was drawn to the creatures. Only after I died did I remember that

I was once a rider and true partner of one of these magnificent beasts. We fought together then. She still exists in another realm; for the moment, we must fight for good separately."

Greg could ask no more as the dream faded into nothingness.

❧❧❧❧

Aisha was a tad surprised when she realized that the shoulder on which her head rested was not that of her husband. At some level, she was aware it was a dream, but it had more of the feel of the altered reality of the out-of-body experiences she had known so often. She sat up and looked at the face of the woman beside her.

"Kadijah!" Aisha called. "You've come."

"I've been here all along, my child," the spirit answered as she held Aisha in a motherly embrace.

"Why has it been so long since you've spoken to me?" Aisha asked.

"Because you had work to do, and I dared not distract you."

"Is the work done then?" Aisha asked.

"This part, at least. I am proud of you, my daughter. You have worked magic, created a healing like no other has accomplished before you."

"I have?"

Kadijah laughed. "Yes, my dear, and now it's time for that magic to go out into the world."

❧❧❧❧

The blare of a ringing phone made the sleeping

couple jump, with Greg nearly falling to the floor from where he was slumped on the loveseat. Greg grabbed for the phone on the end table, succeeding in dropping the cordless receiver once before he finally retrieved and answered it on the fourth ring.

"Hello," Greg said. Aisha listened to his side of the conversation. "Yes, I sent you the JPEGs of Aisha's latest work." Lengthy pause. "I'll have to discuss it with Aisha, hold on a minute." Greg put the receiver against his shoulder. He spoke to Aisha. "I sent some photos of your new paintings to that big Santa Fe Gallery you love. He wants you to bring as many as you want to the gallery so that he can schedule a show. Also, he asks if you would mind if he shipped some for display and sale to affiliates in New York and LA."

Aisha looked at Greg, surprised. "Well, she did say it was time for the magic to go out into the world."

"Who said that?" Greg asked.

"Kadijah."

Greg shook his head, willing the sleep to leave his mind. He smiled before returning the phone to his ear.

"We can ship some paintings to you by the end of the week." Pause. "We'll work out the details later," Greg said. There was a pause and Greg laughed. "Yes, we trust you to be fair. We knew you'd be calling." Another pause. "How? Um, you wouldn't believe me if I told you." Pause again. "Thanks, and we look forward to meeting you in person as soon as we can make it to Santa Fe. Goodbye."

As Greg hung up the phone, Aisha picked up a piece of cantaloupe Greg had left on his plate and popped it in her mouth. "A road trip sounds wonderful," she said. "In the meantime, what else do we have good in the kitchen?"

Greg brushed a strand of hair back from her forehead. "Forget the kitchen, let's go for pizza."

Aisha laughed. "Pizza! Yes, pizza."

She barely had time to brush her hair and change from her paint-stained shirt before Greg ushered her out the door.

Chapter Seven

Betrayal

Kidwell lifted the pot lid and breathed deeply of the aromatic steam escaping from the bubbling concoction. She had to admit that artichoke chicken was one of her favorite dishes to both prepare and eat. Anna would be back soon from her weekly excursion to town. Kidwell had declined to accompany her lover, instead plotting a surprise. The ringers were off the house phone, and her cell and computer screens were cold and blank. Martin had clear instructions she was not to be disturbed. He had smirked happily, as he realized what was afoot, causing Kidwell to blush a deep crimson.

A linen cloth covered the dining table, and the best china and silver were already set. Candles were placed in the candlesticks, waiting for Anna to return before Kidwell put match to wick. A bottle of New Mexico's own Vivac Chardonnay and two perfectly shaped flans chilled in the refrigerator. Kidwell felt as excited as she had on her first date with Anna so many years before. She had showered, taking extra time to make herself as attractive as possible, including the selection of the silk shirt Anna loved to both see and feel, and the perfume she knew Anna loved. Kidwell dreamed, desperately hoped, that Anna would share the excitement once she opened the door and saw the surprise awaiting her.

As soon as Kidwell heard Anna's truck pull into the drive, she rushed outside, opening the driver's door, taking Anna's hand to pull her gently from the vehicle. Anna looked surprised, checking Kidwell from head to toe.

"You're all dressed up. Did I forget something?" she asked.

"Can't a woman dress up if she feels like it?" Kidwell responded, smiling.

One eyebrow raised speculatively as Anna answered. "Yes, I suppose so."

Both women walked to the passenger side of the truck, and managed to carry several bags of groceries in a single trip from truck to the still open kitchen door. Anna stopped just inside, breathing deeply, sniffing the air.

"Artichoke chicken," she said.

"And flan for dessert," Kidwell answered, closing the door behind her.

Anna peeked around the corner into the dining room, seeing the table and all its finery. A sly smile brightened her face. "I thought you stayed home because you were busy."

"I was," Kidwell answered. "You don't think a dinner like this happens by magic, do you?"

Anna put her bags of groceries on the counter and turned to face Kidwell. The *latina* placed her hands on each side of her lover's face and kissed her, long, slow, and sweet. Kidwell unceremoniously dropped the bags she held onto the floor and returned the kiss, wrapping her arms around Anna's waist.

Anna was breathless when she finally spoke, her face nestled against her lover's cheek. "You have me at a disadvantage, *Querida*. I'm disheveled and dirty from a day's work."

Kidwell laughed, giving Anna another quick kiss. "Go shower and change while I put away groceries and make a salad."

Anna's eyes sparkled like they had not done for some time as she swatted Kidwell playfully on the behind, laughing as she ran toward the stairs, heading to their master bedroom to ready herself for the evening ahead.

A tuneless whistle filled the kitchen as Kidwell donned an apron, put away groceries, and continued preparing the special dinner. She put refrigerator rolls in the oven to heat, tore lettuce, and cut up tomatoes and olives to go in the salad before mixing homemade honey/Dijon dressing. She could hear the shower run, and Anna singing as she washed, dried her hair, and dressed. Kidwell was lighting the candles as Anna came down the stairs, wearing a flowing summer dress that she had not worn for a very long time. As Kidwell watched her lover descend the stairs, she felt breathless, as newly in love as the moment when their gazes first met and two old souls recognized the mate of many lives. Kidwell still remembered that moment with awe. It had been as if her whole world shifted on its axis, and she knew as she had never known before that she was not alone, that she had found, as they said in the Carolinas, her "split-apart."

It was like old times as they filled plates, poured wine, laughing and talking over their meal, holding hands and gentle touches accenting the evening. Life had come at them too hard and fast since Kidwell's return from Mexico, and, for the first time, they had an opportunity to share together those experiences each had known separately. Kidwell told of the laughter of half-naked children in the Mayan village, and the resilience of childhood happiness in what most Americans would consider abject poverty. Anna told of her encounter in the grocery store with the older gentleman who cornered her by the coffee aisle, insisting he would not let her leave until she'd agreed to have dinner with him. Anna simply agreed and then made her way rapidly to the freezer section as soon as he stepped away and took a pen from his pocket to take her phone number. He had watched, stunned, as she smiled and waved a goodbye. Anna held Kidwell's hand so tightly that the knuckles of both their hands turned white as Kidwell described the terror of being bound and hauled away by the minions of the drug lord and then laughed in joy as Kidwell told of her magical escape and her time in the past days of a Mayan city.

All was right with their world as they moved on to dessert and coffee. The pieces of their relationship had once again found their place and a mending was underway. A pause filled the house with a comfortable silence. Anna turned suddenly somber, and Kidwell squeezed her hand.

"What is it?" Kidwell asked. "You have something deep on your mind. I've seen the flicker of it behind your eyes. Tell me."

Anna gave a shaky sigh. "I'm afraid, *Querida*."

"Afraid? You who managed to give your kidnapper a black eye even after you were bound and gagged."

"Yes, sweetheart. Afraid, I'm afraid I—" Anna's words were interrupted as a loud knock came at the kitchen door.

"Who the hell can that be?" Kidwell asked. "I

told Martin to field any visitors, and I forwarded the office phone to him. Go on, Anna. Ignore them. This is important."

The knock came again. "No, Kidwell. I cannot speak of this with someone waiting at the door."

Kidwell sat, seriously considering what to do. Another knock came, more urgent. She sighed. "It could be something serious, I guess."

Anna sighed in resignation. "Answer. Let's get it over."

Kidwell walked from the dining room to the kitchen and opened the door. Standing boldly outside was Celia. Kidwell's mouth tightened into a grim line.

"What do you want?" Kidwell asked.

"I ran into Mella Trujillo down the road. I thought you'd want to know her grandson is really sick with pneumonia. She asked if you would come do a blessing."

"How sick is he?"

"It's bad, really bad," Celia answered.

Kidwell thought of Mella and Reuben Trujillo. They were good neighbors and good friends. She remembered the grandson, sickly compared to the rest of the family, plagued with asthma. A lung infection could be serious indeed.

Anna walked up behind Kidwell, and put her hands on her lover's waist. "I heard," Anna said. There was a note of disappointment in her voice. "It's Mella and Reuben. You have to go."

Kidwell turned to Anna and smiled. The energy of connection between them was so strong there was the smell of ozone in the air.

"Can I come in?" Celia asked. "It's a little chilly out here."

Kidwell's smile turned to a frown as she faced the intruder, but Anna answered. "Of course, come on in," she said.

Reluctantly, Kidwell stepped to the side, allowing Celia to enter.

Anna reached into the hanging basket over the counter where they kept car keys. "Take my truck. It's closer," Anna said. "Do you want me to go with you?"

Kidwell gazed into Anna's eyes. "As much as I would enjoy the company, I'm afraid it would be a distraction."

Anna handed Kidwell the keys. "Give them all my love," Anna said. She leaned toward Kidwell and they exchanged a brief kiss. At the sight, Celia turned away uncomfortably.

Kidwell opened the door wide, looking expectantly at Celia, obviously waiting for her to leave. "Thanks for the message. I'll let the Trujillos know you delivered it."

Celia shuffled uncomfortably from foot to foot before she reluctantly exited the kitchen ahead of Kidwell.

"I'll be back as soon as I can," Kidwell said to Anna, kissing her again, a kiss of greater length and passion now that they had privacy.

"Thank you, *Querida*," Anna said.

"For what?"

Anna motioned toward the table where the candles now burned low. "For this, for loving me."

"Anna, I know that when we got together, you didn't bargain for…"

Anna put her fingers to Kidwell's lips. A troubled cloud darkened the light in her eyes. "Shh, Kid. Neither of us knew what would come. We will deal with it as we can."

❧❧❧❧

The warmth of the evening turned cold as the door clicked closed behind Kidwell. Anna stared at that door for several minutes, ceasing to fight the tears that begged for escape. She stood still and silent, tears filling her eyes until one trickled down her cheek and dropped off her chin to leave a dark splotch on the green cotton of her dress. Anna had been so close, so close to telling Kidwell her deepest fear, one that left her very soul cold and paralyzed. Deep inside herself, she knew the healing would not begin until she shared that fear and knew beyond a doubt that Kidwell was by her side as she faced that formless monster.

She saw a shadow approach through the curtained glass of the kitchen door. Anna was surprised at the relief she felt, hoping that some miracle had cancelled Kidwell's mission, and she had returned. As the knock on the door convinced her it was not Kidwell, she hoped instead for the comforting presence of Martin, a young man who was like a son to both Anna and Kidwell. She was disappointed when she opened the door. Celia stood outside.

"Hi," Celia said. "It's too quiet over at my apartment, and I thought you might want some help cleaning up the kitchen. Looks like Kidwell really left a mess."

Anna was momentarily miffed at the woman's implied criticism of Kidwell, but she felt too much relief at the prospect of company to turn the woman away. She opened the door wider and stepped to the side.

"Come in," Anna said. "I would like some company."

Celia was helpful as they gathered and washed dishes and put away food. Celia filled the silence chatting about the horses and the grounds, talking about little things like worming and mowing and repairs needed. The comfort of small talk eased Anna's pain, and she found herself laughing at Celia's tale of the antics of a ground squirrel she could not convince to move out of the hay shed. Celia was as charming as the first day they met, when Celia arrived like a miracle to help during a day of disasters. That day persuaded Anna to hire the groundskeeper.

"Thank you for the help," Anna said. "It's always a long evening here alone when Kidwell is called away."

Celia's motions were angry as she hung a damp dishtowel on the rack. "Seems to me, Kidwell doesn't know what's important."

Anna laughed at that. "I fear the burdens placed on her make the rest of our 'importants' look pretty insignificant."

Celia looked defiantly into Anna's eyes. "Well, she doesn't seem to think you're important."

"Enough!" Anna said with a flash of anger. "What is between Kidwell and me is none of your concern."

Celia backed down immediately, looking at her own boots. "Sorry, I said too much." She reverted quickly from angry to charming. "I like company on these long evenings, too. Thank you for letting me help."

"Yes," Anna responded, still with a hint of anger in her voice. "But I am tired now. Perhaps you had best go home. I want to go to bed and read. It always takes me a little longer to sleep when Kidwell's gone."

Celia smiled brightly. "I can help with that. My mother gets me special tea from the local *curendera*. It always helps when I can't sleep."

Anna looked at the other woman, wondering the motivations of the offer. She decided to take it as an olive branch from Celia for having offended Anna.

"That might help," Anna answered.

Celia motioned toward her barn apartment. "Come on up. I'll fix you a bag of the tea to take home, or perhaps we could visit over a cup."

Anna hesitated, but the thought of being alone at that moment was overwhelming. "Okay, but I can't stay long," she said.

They walked across the yard, pausing to admire the full moon where it hung half-hidden behind silvery clouds. Anna looked at the moon and remembered with a joyful pain those years when it was just her and Kidwell. During the full moon, they almost always sat beneath the stars, playing flute and drum to honor the Moon Goddess. Neither of them had even thought of this full moon, or at least she hadn't. Anna wondered briefly if that had been part of Kidwell's plan for the evening.

Celia led the way up the outside staircase to her apartment above the barn. She smiled as she opened the door and ushered Anna inside. Anna paused, looking around. She hadn't been inside the apartment since the builders had finished, and she was pleased at the homey feel to the little one-bedroom living space.

"Are you comfortable here?" Anna asked.

"Very," Celia answered.

"We worried some that it would smell too much of horse, being over the barn," Anna said.

Celia laughed. "Not much; besides, that's perfume

to me." She motioned toward the couch that was the only place to sit in the living room. "Have a seat. I'll fix you that tea, and put some in a container for you to take home."

Anna started to point out that she hadn't agreed to stay for tea, but decided it would be rude. As she walked toward the couch, she paused briefly, sniffing the air. There was an unpleasant smell, but it wasn't manure or decaying hay. She couldn't quite identify it, and it was too vague to make her uncomfortable. Once seated on the couch, she forgot the smell as she looked through the magazines on the coffee table before her. *American Horse, Horse Illustrated*, every publication was somehow connected to the animals that gave Celia great joy. Anna picked up a catalogue of tack and veterinary products and leafed through, as Celia heated water and poured herbs in a teapot in the kitchen just a few feet away. When Celia walked to her, holding two steaming mugs, Anna was absorbed in photos and descriptions of lightweight trail saddles. Admiring the saddles was intertwined with fantasies of her and Kidwell heading back to Thunder Lake, initiating new saddles and renewing old flames.

"Nice stuff in that catalogue," Celia said as she handed Anna a mug.

"Yes, it is," Anna answered. She put the catalogue back on the table and took a sip of the hot liquid. It was pleasant but earthy in flavor, obviously not some commercial blend boxed and sold by the millions. "This is good."

"Mom swears by it," Celia said. She cleared her throat. "If you don't mind me asking, when I came to your house, it looked to me like you had something major on your mind."

Anna blew across the top of her mug and took another drink. The effect of the tea was pleasant, comforting. "Yes, I did. I was about to tell Kidwell something I've worried about for a long time."

Celia set her mug on the table and turned on the couch to face Anna. "Well, I'm a good listener."

Anna said nothing, feeling herself relax deeply as she drank more of the tea. "I should talk with Kidwell."

"It's on your mind now, and Kidwell's not here. It would be like denying yourself medicine you need because it didn't come from the right doctor."

Anna slumped and laid her head back on the couch. Unbidden, the tears returned. As the relaxation continued to exude throughout her body, she felt her reserve, her control relax as well.

"I…I'm afraid I don't have what it takes to be a prophet's wife," Anna said, and tears abruptly turned to sobs.

Celia moved next to her, putting her arms around the crying woman, and Anna did not have the strength or the desire to move away. The embrace was so comforting, and the unpleasant smell she'd noticed earlier returned, but it seemed different, oddly appealing, even with an aphrodisiac effect. At the edge of her consciousness, she noticed a darkness that hung like a shadow in an upper corner of the room and grew until the whole room darkened in shadow. When Celia kissed her, Anna had lost all will to resist, and with no mental or moral decision involved, she rose when Celia took her hand and pulled her toward the bedroom. Both her heart and mind had taken a leave of absence, and only her body called for the pleasure she knew was to come. For all practical purposes, Anna was absent, and an animal piece of the woman simply complied, like a moth seeking the warmth of a flame. The darkness followed them from one room to the other. At some level, if one listened closely, there was a dark and deep laugh – one heard not with the ears but with the soul – a laugh that left the very soul feeling totally cold and empty.

Chapter Eight

Confrontation

Aisha sat bolt upright in bed. Greg jumped too, her movement driving him from deep sleep directly to fight or flight mode. He opened the nightstand drawer, and his hand rested on the pistol inside, remembering Arthur's admonition to be a protector.

"What's wrong?" Greg demanded. "An intruder, another painting inspiration? What?"

Aisha jumped from bed, walked to the closet, and pulled her suitcase from its place on a shelf. She threw it on the bed, opened it, and began throwing clothes inside with little thought as to what she packed.

"Kidwell needs us," Aisha answered.

"What's wrong?"

"I don't know, but she needs us," she said.

"Is Anna okay?" Greg asked.

Aisha paused in her packing, staring into the distance, trying to decipher the unspoken but urgent message she'd heard with heart more than mind. There was anger in her voice when she answered.

"No, she is not."

Greg rose from bed, taking the 9mm pistol from the drawer and leaving it on the nightstand. He planned to pack it. Aisha's urgency told him that he needed to be ready for anything.

❧❧❧❧❧

Martin laid in bed, looking at the ceiling, the strange feeling of disquiet that awoke him still teasing at his mind. He threw back the covers and walked to the kitchen of the one-bedroom guesthouse that was his home. Martin hoped a drink of cool well water would quiet the discomfort. He looked through the window at a moonlit night and was surprised to see lights on not only in the kitchen of the main house but also in the bedroom of Celia's apartment over the barn. As he looked, shadows appeared behind the curtain of the apartment. Two moved together into an embrace so passionate that Martin felt embarrassment at being an accidental voyeur. He felt an unwanted certainty that he knew who it was, and his heart felt as cold as the well water forgotten in the glass he held.

❧❧❧❧❧

Kidwell was tired beyond words as she pulled into the yard and parked beside the house. The blessing had helped, but Kidwell was not surprised that Celia had exaggerated the situation. The boy had a bad cold turning into bronchitis. Mella and Rueben had been happy and surprised to see Kidwell, especially so late. Mella shook her head in frustration when Kidwell said that Celia had delivered a message that said she was urgently needed.

"Urgent!" Mella exclaimed. "I ran into that… that woman at the post office this afternoon and just mentioned that Juan was sick."

Kidwell frowned. "Yes. I see."

"Kidwell, don't trust her," Mella said. The older

woman whispered so that Rueben, in the kitchen making coffee, couldn't hear. "If you ask me, she's after your Anna."

Kidwell laughed bitterly. "I know. Her time at our place is coming to an end, especially after this."

Since she was there, Kidwell performed the healing blessing, just as White Buffalo Calf Woman had taught her. As she blew smoke, said the words, and covered the boy in the incense of sage and sweet grass, his breathing eased, and he slept quietly. Kidwell's irritation at Celia eased as she realized the visit was helping the boy. She didn't stay long after the ceremony was complete. All she wanted was to go home.

As Kidwell stepped out of the truck and walked toward the kitchen, she was surprised to see the lights still on. She thought Anna would be in bed. For all the world, all Kidwell wanted to do was put on her pajamas and curl up beside her sleeping lover.

"Kidwell," Martin said from the darkness.

Kidwell jumped and swore like the sailor she was.

"Geeze, Martin. You scared the hell out of me," Kidwell said. Martin stepped into the light from the porch, and Kidwell felt a different kind of fear as she saw the pallor of his face. "What's wrong? Is Anna okay?"

Martin swallowed hard. "Kid...I..."

"Where's Anna?" Kidwell demanded.

Martin's mouth opened, but no sound came out. Instead, he looked toward the light in the bedroom window of Celia's apartment.

It took a minute for the meaning of the situation to sink fully into Kidwell's consciousness. When it did, she stood stunned, fighting to breathe.

"No," Kidwell said. "She wouldn't do that."

"Kid, go inside. I'll talk to them," Martin answered.

"No, no. It's not true." Kidwell ran into her own house, up the stairs, and to the bedroom that she shared with Anna. The bed was empty, still neatly made from that morning. The chicken dinner she'd so enjoyed earlier in the evening suddenly revolted, and Kidwell rushed to the bathroom, ridding herself of the meal but not of the cold fear that now consumed her.

"Kidwell," Martin called gently from the stairwell. "You okay?"

Kidwell splashed cold water on her face at the sink and looked in the mirror, frightened at the whiteness of her own face. It was like looking at her own ghost. Perhaps it was. She felt as if all life had been sucked out of her, like the essence of living was gone and all that was left was the motion of physical animation. Then the passion of terror returned, and she had to know, to see for herself.

Kidwell rushed down the stairs, barely noticing Martin as she flew past, taking the steps two at a time. She didn't remember crossing the yard with Martin in her wake, nor hear his voice as he begged her to be calm, to think. Kidwell rushed up the outside stairway to the barn apartment and used the master key on her key ring to open the door, Martin right behind her. As she stepped into the air of the room, Kidwell had to cover her nose with the sleeve of her shirt because of the stench of darkness. She saw as well as felt the cloud of a demon filling the entire space. Unseen but suddenly felt, White Buffalo Calf Woman was beside her, and, for a moment, Kidwell felt a deep calm. She raised her hand and waved it in an arch, feeling White Buffalo Calf Woman moving with her.

"Be gone, never to return here," Kidwell said, and a soundless scream filled the space as the demon imploded with a pop, replacing the stench with the scent of clean air.

Celia stood naked beside the bedroom door. The sneer she'd worn on her face earlier was still in place, but her eyes were filled with surprise and confusion. The naked woman shook her head, appearing to seek the bravado she'd felt in the presence of the demon, the one she'd never recognized but that had ruled her for so long. What remained were her own feelings of being cheated, of injustice, feelings that had given the demon an inroad to her heart and mind in the first place.

"You're too late," Celia said.

Kidwell felt Martin's arms wrap around her from behind, strong but gentle.

"Don't kill her," he whispered. "She's not worth it."

Kidwell understood Martin's fear, and she looked at the naked woman, surprised at her own feelings. There was no hate, anger, yes, but more pity than anything else. Martin was right. She wasn't worth it. Kidwell patted Martin's hands lovingly and gently loosened his grip. She walked up to Celia and looked her in the eye, feeling no joy at the fear that caused Celia to raise her fists and back into a corner.

"Get dressed and leave," Kidwell said, amazingly calm. "Don't come back. We'll pack your things and send them to you along with your final paycheck."

Martin tossed a throw from the back of the couch to Celia.

"Cover yourself," he said. He turned to Kidwell. "I'll handle her," he said, jerking his head toward a now cowering Celia, contempt dripping from his voice. "Go to…" He couldn't bring himself to say the name of the other woman who was like a mother to him.

Kidwell left the room, cold with fear at what she'd find when she entered the bedroom. Anna lie sobbing on the bed, covers pulled tightly around her chin. The summer dress she'd worn earlier lay rumpled on the floor beside her. Anna took a deep breath, striving to control her crying, and she looked at Kidwell with a hint of defiance. Kidwell walked slowly to the bed and sat tentatively on the edge, longing to reach out to Anna and just a little afraid that, if she did so, it would be to slap the woman whom she loved more than any other person.

"Anna," Kidwell nearly choked on her tears. "Why?"

Anna turned her gaze to the bed, not looking at Kidwell. "I don't know. It just happened."

"What–" Kidwell sat staring at her hands, gathering the strength to ask the next question. "– What do you think we should do now?"

Anna mumbled into the pillow. "I don't know. I don't think I can live like…like we have."

Kidwell closed her eyes, tears streaming past the closed lids. "Anna, answer this honestly. Do you want to be with me?"

Anna took a shaky breath, and glanced tentatively at Kidwell. Her voice could barely be heard, she spoke so quietly. "I don't know."

Kidwell's body jerked involuntarily, as though she'd been punched in the stomach. She took a deep breath and stood. "That's not good enough."

Kidwell walked purposefully toward the bedroom door before she turned to face Anna once again. "I'll leave the keys in your truck, with a packed bag inside as well. When you want to come for more of your things, call Martin to schedule a time. I'll make sure I'm gone."

Anna sat upright, her eyes wide. "Kidwell!" she called, but it was too late. Kidwell was already out the front door and halfway down the steps.

Martin called after her, but Kidwell barely paused, yelling back at him from the yard. "I need to be alone," she said. Reluctantly, Martin left her alone, opting instead to expedite Celia's departure. He watched as Kidwell entered the main house. A few minutes later, he saw her leave the house and place something in Anna's truck. Then Kidwell was gone, wandering into the darkness of the forest.

❧ ❧ ❧ ❧

Kidwell didn't realize she was heading for the tree she and Anna had always called the fairy throne until she was there. She had no clue how she'd walked through the dark, not stumbling once on the rough path. The ground was cold as she sat where a looping root made a natural throne with the tree itself as the back. Sobs racked Kidwell's body, taking on a life of their own, not under her control or even conscious awareness that they were ready to be released. The years of joy and happiness she had known with Anna flashed before her eyes as though the death of a true love were death itself. There were even the flashes of earlier lives, memories they had both shared.

From the moment she first met Anna, she knew they were meant to be together. Before that time, Kidwell had thought she knew what happiness could be, but only with Anna had she mined the depths of the fullness of life. Kidwell felt as though half her heart had died. As she leaned against the fairy tree, she closed her eyes and felt reality shift. She opened her eyes to a different world. Daylight warmed her and the pine at her back had turned to a cottonwood. Prairie, not forest, now surrounded her. Lakota country, she thought, and she felt calmed, as she knew who was coming.

"You will live, you know," White Buffalo Calf Woman said as she took a seat on the river sand beside Kidwell.

"Right now, I don't want to," Kidwell answered.

The ancient Lakota spirit sat silent, looking to the distance.

"There is more than you now know entwined with the story of you and Anna. The pain you feel, this trial, it may be necessary for many."

"How? If this has purpose, maybe I can bear it," Kidwell responded.

The spirit woman caressed Kidwell's face, like a mother comforting a child. "I cannot take away your pain, but know that you are not alone and that the journey through this pain will give you what you need to bear the burden that is yours."

Kidwell moved to lay flat in the sun-warmed sand. The warmth offered some small comfort.

"There's more?" Kidwell asked. "Dear God, how much can I bear? Now I understand what Jesus meant when he asked God to take this burden from him."

"Not yet, not totally, but you will. Feel the pain, my child, but know that you will live through this journey and find your soul in a place that few ever reach. There is a gift to come. I promise."

Kidwell drifted into a troubled sleep and awoke, shivering. She was once again in the cool of the mountains. She rose and began the walk home, to her empty home and her empty bed. Despite the rose-colored glow of a sunrise, this time she stumbled as she walked.

Chapter Nine

Into the Darkness

When Aisha and Greg pulled into the yard, it was mid-morning. They had driven through the darkness, completing the five-hour drive to arrive by 9 a.m. Aisha had been so anxious that they had barely stopped for gasoline along with breakfast sandwiches and coffee to go. Martin stepped out of the barn where he was finishing the morning tasks of caring for animals. As soon as the couple saw the dejected posture of the proud young man, any doubt they may have had concerning Aisha's premonition disappeared. As soon as Aisha stepped out the passenger-side door, Martin picked her up off the ground in a bear hug.

"Thank God, you're here," the young man said. "How did you know to come? Did Kidwell call?"

"I love you too, Martin, but please put me down. I can't breathe," Aisha responded.

"What's going on?" Greg asked as he stood beside the car.

"You don't know?" Martin responded.

"I know I woke in the night, my heart cold with fear, knowing Kidwell and Anna were in trouble," Aisha responded.

Greg walked around the car and put his hands on Martin's shoulders. "We've imagined every scenario in the world," he said. "What's wrong? Were they in a wreck? Did Kidwell get sick from some bug she picked up in Mexico? Did one of the crazies come to hurt them? Tell us!"

Martin leaned against the car and took a shaky breath. "I doubt you imagined this," he said. "I never, ever would have thought it possible."

Aisha and Greg listened in shocked silence as Martin recounted the events of the prior night. When he was done, they broke their silence with disbelieving questions – about Celia, Anna's state of mind, how it all could come to be. Martin answered as best he could, but none of them could imagine what could have happened in Anna's mind and heart.

"Where is Kidwell?" Aisha demanded.

"Up in their, I mean, her room," Martin answered. "I checked on her a couple of hours ago. She didn't answer when I called from downstairs, so I went up. She told me she'd be fine and to just leave her alone. She asked me to take care of the horses, which I was going to do anyway."

Aisha turned to the house. Martin started to follow, but Greg stopped him.

"Leave them. Aisha will know far more about what to do than either of us. Help me take our bags inside."

While the two men carried luggage from car to house, Aisha walked up the steps and into Kidwell's room. Aisha's concern almost turned to panic as she saw the strongest person she had ever known curled into a fetal position on the bed.

"Kid," Aisha said, almost a whisper.

Kidwell rolled over and looked at her co-prophet. "Aisha?" She leaned on one elbow, facing the other woman. "How did you know?"

"That you needed us?" Aisha gave a slightly bitter laugh. "Kidwell, you of all people should know that we don't need phone calls or emails to know when the other is in crisis."

Kidwell still looked at Aisha, her face and position unchanged, but tears welled in her eyes and drifted quietly down her cheeks. "Did Martin tell you that—?"

"Yes, he told us what happened."

"Anna…she…Aisha, I don't know that I have the heart to live without her," Kidwell said, her voice cracking at the end.

Aisha sat on the bed and pulled Kidwell's head into her lap, stroking her friend, her soul sister's hair. "You will live, for it is not ours to choose when we take our first breath nor our last, at least not for a person like you."

"White Buffalo Calf Woman told me that there would be a gift in the pain," Kidwell said.

"She is never wrong."

"But I have lost half my heart. How can I survive that kind of pain?"

"I can't answer that," Aisha said. "I don't know how. I just know that you will."

As Aisha stroked her hair, the dam of emotion that Kidwell had fought to control burst, and sobs racked her body as she cried as she had never cried in her whole life. The pain was so palatable that Aisha cried with her, feeling a piece of the pain that racked her friend's very soul. In time, there were no more tears to cry. Kidwell lay still, her breath shaky but coming more slowly and easily. In the pause, Aisha moved slightly, easing the mild cramp in her thigh stemming from the awkward position she'd assumed and held, unwilling to disturb Kidwell's sorrow. When she moved, Aisha's gaze fell on the wall beside the bed and the painting on rough wood that she saw there. A sharp intake of breath showed her surprise, a surprise profound enough that it even penetrated Kidwell's sorrow.

Kidwell sat up. "What is it?" she asked.

"The painting, the one of the eye, where did you get it?" Aisha asked.

"In Mexico City at a street market. It called to me. Why?"

Aisha laughed softly. "I painted that when I was still a girl, back in Iraq before my family immigrated to Canada."

"What?"

"How do you suppose it got to Mexico?" Aisha asked.

"I have no idea," Kidwell responded. "I just knew I had to have it as soon as I saw it."

Aisha touched Kidwell's face, feeling the drying salt of her friend's tears. "Have you had anything to eat or drink?"

Kidwell thought for a moment. "I honestly don't know. I don't think so, not since—" There was a long painful pause. "—not since last night."

"I'm going to make you some tea and toast," Aisha said.

"I'm really not…"

"I don't care if you don't want it. You will eat and drink," Aisha demanded.

Kidwell simply nodded in compliance. She knew Aisha was right and didn't have the energy to argue. As Aisha left the room, Kidwell stared at the painting she'd named Dragon's Eye. After a moment, she could have sworn she saw the eye blink and turn its gaze fully upon her. Kidwell laughed humorlessly, amazed at how deeply the grief was affecting her very senses. Even through the grief, she felt curious and rose from the bed to stand before the painting. Much to her surprise, the eye continued to look alive, and Kidwell leaned closer, rubbing her eyes and waiting for the illusion to pass.

Kidwell was not unaccustomed to shifts in reality, but she felt a sensation unlike anything she'd known before. She felt drunk, not inebriated but like water in a glass, as her entire being became fluid, rushing toward and then through the eye. She lost consciousness as she felt her feet leave the floor.

Chapter Ten

Metamorphosis

Kidwell awoke slowly, the oddly comforting feel of cold stone beneath her. Her brain was on overload, and she came to consciousness gradually, the body as well as the mind striving to process both the flood of emotion that had overwhelmed her and the inexplicable events following her study of the Dragon's Eye. Altered reality was part of her normal world, but she had never experienced such a drastic metamorphosis, especially on the heels of great personal trauma. When she first opened her eyes, she couldn't see what was around her, not only because of hazy vision following unconsciousness but also because the surroundings were so unfamiliar that her mind had no frame of reference to give what she saw meaning. Then, her eyes and her mind began to clear, and she looked at the stone floor.

She saw a four-fingered, clawed hand right beside her, covered in black scales, iridescent with the hint of rainbow. In that moment, she felt blind terror, and a scream escaped without any conscious decision to make a sound. Her panic only increased at the roar so close that it echoed in her skull, and she scurried backwards, walking on hands as well as feet, trying to escape the giant creature. She didn't stop until she hit a wall of the large, airy cavern where she found herself. Kidwell's breath came in ragged gasps, and she saw tendrils of smoke floating upward, right in front of her face. Finally, the long habits of coping she'd so well developed in her life took hold, and she calmed, that part of her mind that always took charge in crisis giving her the grace and peace she needed to think.

Kidwell swallowed the panic she felt as she raised her hand before her face and realized the clawed appendage was her very own. The tendrils of smoke were a part of her very breath. She looked at her surroundings, and she saw what she somehow already knew to be the bedchamber of a dragon. Carved into the side of a mountain, a large shelf was covered in sheepskins and straw to form a very presentable bed. A large basin carved into the floor had water running slowly from an artesian spring into a pool. The pool had an overflow that trickled in a channel cut into the floor until the water flowed in that same channel beneath a pair of huge, wooden doors with a smaller, human-sized door inset into the right-hand side. Kidwell tentatively stood on all fours and walked hesitantly toward the pool. In the gentle waters, she could see her reflection and confirmed her own face was now that of a massive dragon. Her face and body were an odd black color with hints of rainbow, like the feathers of a raven in sunlight. The face, one she didn't remember seeing, seemed frighteningly familiar. She felt a wave of almost memories so intense that she had an attack of vertigo and had to lie flat on the floor, waiting for the dizziness to pass.

She looked as best she could toward her own back and noted the absence of wings, but still felt certain that she knew the sensation of flight. *I'm a Chinese dragon*, she realized. Her flight came not from the physical power of wings, but from the old, deep magic of dragons. Kidwell had no clue how she knew this, but she accepted it as fact.

The pool before her called to her, and she lowered her snout into the water and drank deeply, sucking in moisture much as her horses did from stream or trough. As Kidwell looked around, she saw a strange eye-shaped mirror not hanging *on* the stone but a part of the stone on the wall near where she first awoke. It wasn't the solid glass of a standard mirror, but the reflective surface had more of the appearance of mercury. She rose to look at the mirror and, behind her own reflection, she could see the ghostly image of her bedroom back in New Mexico. Kidwell sat on her haunches, totally flummoxed. She had no idea where she was, who she was, nor a clue what to do next.

At the far end of the chamber, there was another pair of huge doors, not as sturdy as the ones she assumed were exterior doors. Abruptly, the interior doors flew open and two dragons entered in haste. They were both large-bodied dragons with impressive wings folded against their bodies. One was smaller and sleeker, far younger in appearance. An odd cry escaped the lips of the older dragon, and she rushed toward Kidwell, but when Kidwell instinctively pulled away, the other dragon stopped and sat on a great wooden platform that apparently sufficed as a chair.

From mind-to-mind, the other dragon spoke in a language Kidwell understood. She had no clue as to how she knew that language, but it felt oddly comfortable in her mind. Great tears welled into the older dragon's eyes and fell to the stone floor with a mild hiss as the hot tears hit cold stone.

Welcome home, Sister, the dragon said telepathically.

It was too much. Kidwell fainted.

Chapter Eleven

Memories

Hunger finally woke her. Kidwell rested on the massive platform dragon bed in the same chamber where she'd lost consciousness. She raised herself on one arm and saw the younger of the two dragons who had greeted her earlier curled up and snoozing on the floor beside the platform. Kidwell's mind was still a muddle of confusion, but she found the surroundings oddly familiar, and she had flashes of memory like those she had known when remembering past lives, but more profound.

"I don't know you," Kidwell mumbled in her physical dragon voice, using the language she remembered but had no recollection of ever learning. "I should know you," she continued, speaking softly to the sleeping dragon.

The younger dragon blinked sleepily. "No, you shouldn't," she answered. "I was hatched long after you chose a human existence."

"Then you are?"

"Your niece, Allana. I'm barely a hatchling, only alive for one-hundred fifty-three revolutions of the earth around the sun, but I've watched you for three of your human lives." She motioned with her snout at the mercury-like, eye-shaped view screen of Kidwell's human world. "I have been proud to be your niece,

Aunt Harrana."

The name hit Kidwell like a slap. It had been her name once – long, long ago. She wasn't ready to embrace that existence, not yet.

"Please, please call me Kidwell."

The younger dragon said Kidwell's human name aloud, but the word seemed alien as it fell from her tongue. "I shall try," the young dragon said. "I have heard you called that many times through the portal."

The hunger that awakened Kidwell was still there. When her dragon stomach growled in emptiness, the sound echoed off the stone walls. Young Allana giggled, a sound more like water running over stones than the soft sound of a young girl laughing. Allana closed her eyes and bowed her head, and Kidwell realized she was sending a telepathic message.

"Mother will bring food," Allana said.

Kidwell looked around. "Is this your weyr?"

"Yes, but you can stay here as long as you want. Mother's space is quite large, and I shall stay with her while you're here. I hope you are here for a very long time."

The interior door opened, and Allana's mother entered, carrying a large basket woven from saplings and holding a variety of melons, greens, and meat, even a few sulfurous smelling stones. Kidwell was amazed at the longing her dragon body felt at the sight of the food, especially the huge chunks of meat. Her mind might still be human, but her body was fully dragon.

"Thank you, Sister," Kidwell said. She looked long at the older blue dragon, flashes of memory flooding her, including her time as a young dragon just hatched from an egg brought from the East and adopted by the family of Western dragons. "Thank you, Masat," she said, as she remembered not only her sister's name but also flashes of many wonderful times together, but she was too hungry to dwell on those memories.

Kidwell demolished the food in a matter of minutes, belching deeply and unashamedly when she was done. Dragon manners were different, and such habits were easy to recall and practice.

"How long have I slept?" Kidwell asked.

"A full turning of the sun," Masat answered.

Kidwell jumped up, stepping off the platform and rushing toward the mercurial portal. "My friends," Kidwell exclaimed. "They must be frantic."

"Rest easy, Sister. The portals were developed after the veil was closed, following the great battle. We have used them to monitor the progress, or lack thereof, of humanity, but they are portals of time as well as space. When or if you wish to return, I can say the spells and you can choose not only the place but also the time. If you wish, it can be only moments after your departure." Masat laughed a deep rumble. "We placed one in Allana's chamber because from the time she was hatched she has been fascinated with her aunt who chose to be human. There are natural viewing portals near your home, but it has been a great joy for us all when you found the eye and placed it within your very weyr."

Allana became excited. "Yes, all dragons know what you did and that—"

Masat glared at her daughter, silencing the younger dragon.

"All in good time," Masat said. "You must be confused and tired."

Kidwell sat on her haunches. For a moment, a very old and unwanted memory struggled for life. She saw Anna's face from another lifetime, a helmet of leather and iron covering her head and her beautiful face contorted in tears and grief. Kidwell's mind swallowed the memory, unable to go further, and Kidwell struggled to contain sobs beating at the walls of her chest, begging for escape.

"Go, Allana. Your aunt needs some privacy," Masat said.

Before doing as she was bid, Allana walked to Kidwell, rubbing her snout against her beloved aunt's face and giving a deep rumble that could only be described as a purr. The touch was comforting to Kidwell, but it did not assuage the wave of grief begging for voice.

Allana had no more than closed the door, when hot tears rolled down Kidwell's dragon face, and steam rose as they hit the cold stone of the floor. Masat stood close to her sister. Instinctively, Kidwell leaned her full weight against her dragon sister as the sobs escaped. For hours, it seemed, Masat stood strong, unwavering in the comfort she offered Kidwell. When the sobs had finally eased, Masat led Kidwell to the pool of clear water, insisting she drink and then directed, almost lifted, Kidwell back to the bed platform.

Kidwell lay, stunned, struggling to even identify the cause of the depth of her grief. She was still the woman who had stood beside the painting of a dragon's eye, devastated by the grief of profound betrayal by the person whom she most loved in the whole universe. That pain beating in her dragon heart still sent a deep numbness along her dragon limbs, made each dragon breath a labored struggle. But there was more. There was another grief, a grief beyond time, a grief that made the simple betrayal by her lover seem like child's play. Emotional memories overwhelmed her, feeling as though she grieved for an entire world, for all of existence, but memories of moments were brief flashes, offering little sense or form. Kidwell had been here before. She once told Anna that past life memories were like trying to understand a movie from glimpses of brief and random scenes.

Kidwell saw a green earth rolling beneath her and felt the joy of dragon flight, knowing a deep psychic bond with the woman who rode her, a graceful warrior, her Anna. Kidwell finally comprehended the extent of the bond she had with her soulmate. That psychic bond had the bitter taste of combined fear. They flew to battle.

Another flash, grief so deep it overshadowed the pain of multiple wounds. She looked to see the deep red hair of a weeping woman, a magnificent warrior. She lay across the still body of another dragon, charred and bleeding and obviously without life. Kidwell heard her own dragon voice scream in grief the single word, "Brother!" Anna, still clad in armor of leather and iron, now bloody and burned, lay prostrate a few yards away, sobbing in deep grief and something else, something Kidwell felt through the psychic bond – shame, shame so profound it overshadowed all else.

No more came. The scenes were done, for now. The only complete piece to the memory was emotion, profound and painful. She no longer had the energy to sob and was surprised at the sound of her own moan as she lay upon her dragon bed.

"We will be here, Sister. You need only think my name, and I shall return, and you will survive this grief. You are the strongest of dragons. Not even your own broken heart can defeat you, but this battle may take time."

A loud thump at the exterior door caused Masat to change her focus from Kidwell to the door.

"No, please," Kidwell said as Masat moved to open the door. "I wish to see no one."

"This one you must see, if even for a short time. Maolan has long awaited your return."

The massive doors opened with a groan, and in the doorway stood a resplendent emerald green dragon. The dragon came straight to Kidwell, placing her taloned hands on each of Kidwell's shoulders and leaning her forehead against Kidwell's. The touch felt comforting, and memories stirred of deep affection for an old friend, but something wasn't quite right. Only when she first met Anna had Kidwell felt a recognition so profound.

"Welcome back, dear friend," the new dragon said, a distinct Irish drawl, even in her dragon voice.

"I remember you, but I don't," Kidwell said.

"Perhaps, old friend, it's because the last time you saw me, I was human."

Chapter Twelve

Stasis

It's shock, Kidwell thought as her dragon body curled into a ball, and she placed her face toward the stone wall. She could still think and knew that the sudden loss of all emotion and the sense of cold that enveloped her was emotional overload. She could think but had not the strength to do anything about it. She could hear Maolan and Masat mumbling behind her, but she had not the will to listen, nor the heart to care what they had to say. She drifted into a troubled sleep. It would be a long one.

The same dream came over and over. There was Anna, naked beneath the thin sheet and sobbing as though she grieved to the depths of her soul, then she morphed into another Anna, an earlier Anna, still sobbing, clothed in the leather and shining metal of light armor, and lying face down in the earth. The grief of both sights wove and bobbed within Kidwell's heart and subconscious mind. Somehow, they were tied, those two Annas and the Kidwell who watched them. Sometimes, in the dream of the earlier Anna, Kidwell felt the helpless brokenness of her own body as she tried to drag herself toward the armored Anna, and it was her own dragon hands she saw reaching forward and pulling her toward Anna.

Every time, Kidwell awoke with a groan and

tears in her eyes and on her cheeks. The two images, the two times were somehow intertwined and related, but Kidwell could not yet make sense of it in the hodge-podge of emotions and half-memories that now absorbed her. There was so much that sleep provided the only means her system could deal with the barrage. She had vague memories of Masat or Maolan awakening her with an insistence that she eat or drink, and she learned the path out the door and to the deep ravine that served as outhouse for the weyr, a journey for which she woke herself when the need became insistent.

More than once, she awoke with the comforting presence of her niece curled beside her and realized that the moans from her nightmares had so worried the young dragon that Allana had come to sleep beside her aunt. It helped. Kidwell felt less alone and more closely tied to her long-forgotten dragon family. That feeling of belonging encouraged memories forward. The first clear memories were of her and Masat as young dragons, their first taste of the sulfurous stone that helped charge their inner fires, watching Masat's first flight as she learned to use her wings, and Kidwell's own early efforts to access the magical ability of an Eastern dragon to fly without wings. The ability was tied more to electromagnetic fields than magic, and Kidwell's first flights were accidental as she tapped into a field leading to a path she intended to take. Although the memories came in dreams or in half-waking states, it was like a door slamming shut when a third sibling entered the picture, a great purple dragon, an older brother, and the name Falong brought joy then deep sorrow as it sprung full-blown into Kidwell's befuddled mind.

At the root of it all was deep grief. Anna's

betrayal – the loss of her soulmate – had ripped a hole in Kidwell's universe. Then for a transformation to an alternate reality to follow that, Kidwell slept and slept, her mind and spirit making sense of the pain and the confusion.

Something more was happening, a transformation during this period of stasis. All the bits and pieces of Kidwell's old soul were sorting and processing like pieces of a jigsaw puzzle. Even in the confusion of her inner being, Kidwell knew without the words to explain, even to herself, that this effort toward wholeness could not have begun without the catalyst of deep pain. The pain was like vinegar in baking soda, the catalyst for a dramatic reaction that would have stayed forever dormant without the pain. She saw its importance, but she could not yet feel gratitude for this troubled journey. Her subconscious pieced together the millennium of human lifetimes preceding her present one – as warrior, as healer, as farmer, as sailor, as explorer, as mother, as father, as a thousand children in a thousand lifetimes.

Anna's face, although new in each lifetime, was always welcome. Most were happy times and lives, but there was a recurring theme during those lives of war or hardship. Kidwell never doubted Anna's love, even her courage, to a point. Time and again, when all looked hopeless, Anna doubted herself at that critical moment. There was a grief with each one, and Kidwell wondered why she came back to Anna over and over. It seemed somehow important.

Finally, Kidwell awoke.

She had no clue how many days and nights she had laid there, sleeping and tossing, moaning and crying. In the end, her always-active mind found a force as strong as grief – boredom. The grief was still there, sleeping in the back space of her heart like a sated animal too long indulged. It was the mind that came awake, curiosity alive and looking around the weyr not for essentials of the moment but analytically, searching for purpose and form in the cavern's structure and the simplistic dragon-sized furniture of stone and wood. The feeling of familiarity was stronger now that the millennia of memories had begun to sort and place themselves.

She looked at the ever-flowing pool in her chamber and knew its structure, for she had used and helped build such pools many times before. Mountain homes were chosen for the presence of artesian wells pressured from a system of aquifers. Because of the constant flow both in and out, these pools served for both drinking and bathing, except when the dragons chose to fly to their favorite hot springs, enjoying water that would have parboiled any human. As Kidwell looked at the water, she felt an intense longing, first for a long drink and then for a good soak. She stuck her snout in the pool and drank long and deep, and then she placed her mouth to the large hole, which she knew to be a hollow space beside the pool. From both memory and instinct, she breathed fire, using her own internal furnace to heat the stone, which, in turn, heated the water. Kidwell sat back in surprise. She had no clue that she had that knowledge until she used the skill. Abruptly she wondered if this was what it was like for a normal, garden-variety amnesia patient.

The thought passed, and she returned her mouth to the hole in the stone, one clawed hand in the water, testing temperature. When it was right, she stepped inside, and the overflow splashed into the channels around the pool that then led across the floor and outside the chamber. As Kidwell settled into the water, she felt such a deep pleasure that her mind seemed to vibrate. While still sensitive, she was sure she felt a surprised reply from at least three beings. They were familiar, but she was not yet reacquainted with dragon telepathy to be able to differentiate who was whom.

Beside the pool, there was a stack of sweet smelling leaves, and Kidwell took a handful and systematically scrubbed at her long-unwashed self. When crushed, the leaves emitted soft suds, and the constantly flowing pool gradually swept the soapy water away. Kidwell took a moment to breathe fire into the stone heater once again, renewing the temperature of the ever-flowing pool.

The interior door opened and Allana rushed inside, followed slightly more sedately by her mother and Maolan. *Ah, of course those are the three minds I reached*, Kidwell thought.

Allana gave the soft chortle that Kidwell knew as a young dragon's giggle.

"So, you like my pool?" Allana asked.

"Very much," Kidwell answered.

"Have you decided to join the living, Sister?" Masat asked.

Kidwell stared into her rippling reflection in the water around her. "There were moments I wished to make another choice, but it never was really an option."

Masat looked away, embarrassed. "My apologies, Sister. It was a poor joke."

Kidwell moved to grasp her sister's hand. "No, Masat. You need apologize for nothing. Your love and kindness—" Kidwell paused to look at all three of her companions. "—Your love and kindness kept me here, gave me comfort when I needed it."

Maolan sat beside the pool, looking at her friend. "How much do you remember?"

Kidwell studied the green dragon, still striving to sort the depth of connection she felt with her.

Kidwell shook her head. "Still bits and pieces. It seems I only recall those human lives and moments that are relevant to my development, and I remember many pleasant times in my early dragon centuries, but there's a gap, something I cannot see past."

The emerald scales around Maolan's heart took on a reddish glow, and a tendril of smoke floated up from each nostril. Kidwell recognized an anger with such depth that it smelled of hate.

"And Annalome, was she a part of those lives?" Maolan asked, her voice frightening in its softness.

"In most, perhaps all. Yes, she was," Kidwell answered. Kidwell did not need to ask whom she meant. It was Anna.

Masat intervened. "Enjoy your bath, Sister. Tonight, we will all dine together in the great hall. Come down the hallway when you are done. I feel certain you will remember the way."

The red glow eased in Maolan's chest, and her mood changed. "It has been many millennia since we've shared a feast together, old friend." She laughed. "And this time we will eat from the same bowl instead of my hand on human bread and your fangs deep in the often-raw meat favored by dragons."

The three visitors left, and Kidwell heated the pool one last time, enjoying the hot water. When her body felt clean, a piece of her spirit felt refreshed. In that moment, Kidwell believed that the will to live might yet return to her heart as well as her body.

Chapter Thirteen

Unwelcome

The summer dress Anna had donned with such joy not many hours earlier was now wrinkled and bedraggled. She dressed in it anyway, feeling awkward and out-of-place in Celia's unfamiliar bedroom. There was nothing else available for her to wear. Besides, Anna just didn't care. She swam in a well of emptiness in her soul. Even the movement of her own body felt alien and distant. There was no choice but to leave. Staying would only deepen her shame, her surprise at her own weakness, yet there was a taste of familiarity to this failure, this moment.

Anna slowly descended the steps, making her way to her truck, still parked where Kidwell left it beside the house. For several minutes, she stared longingly at the light shining from the upstairs window. She saw a shadow move across the room and felt as though an icicle were driven through her heart. It was her beloved Kidwell, the most important person in her life. Anna sobbed as she wondered if she would ever again see that beloved face.

"You need to go, Anna," a voice said from the darkness.

Anna turned to see Martin standing in the shadows.

"That woman—" His voice dripped distaste. "—

Already gone."

"Martin, I..." Anna's mouth continued to move, but no words came. She had no idea what to say.

"Just go, Anna, please." In the moonlight, there was a glint of tears on Martin's cheeks. "We'll figure out what to do later. For now, just go."

Anna wiped tears from her eyes. She looked in the back of her pickup and saw her own suitcase, already packed by Kidwell.

"Okay, okay, I'll go." Anna climbed in the truck, started the engine, backed from the drive, and turned around to drive toward the county road. As she turned, she saw Kidwell's shadow move upstairs, and a curtain pulled back slightly. Anna paused, praying Kidwell would open the window and call for her to stop, to come inside so they could talk it through. Instead, the shadow stood, unmoving. Anna put the truck in gear and drove away. She felt as though she were driving to her doom.

When Anna got to the end of the drive, she saw a car parked by the road, its lights off and the engine stopped. It was Celia's car. Anna stopped at the end of the driveway as Celia got out of her car and walked toward her. The bravado Anna had always seen in Celia was gone. There was a hesitation to her steps. Reluctantly, Anna rolled her window down just a few inches.

"I'm sorry," Celia said. She tried to reach through the window to touch Anna, but stopped as Anna glared menacingly. "Where will you go?"

Anna took a deep breath and shook her head. "No idea. A motel, I guess. I can't face any of our friends right now. Oh God! Aisha may kill me."

Celia took a shaky breath. "My parents live at

Trujillo. I'm going there. I think they would welcome you too."

"I don't know," Anna answered.

"Anna, right now, I don't know why I did what I did. Let me at least do this, give you a place to go for now," Celia said.

Anna stared into the darkness of the woods beside the road. She had no clue where to go or what to do. She nodded a weak agreement. At least there was the comfort in having someone else decide her next move, at least for now. Celia went back to her car and Anna followed as Celia started the engine, turned on the lights, and headed down the road.

❧ ❧ ❧ ❧

As they pulled into the yard, there were no lights on in the house. Anna looked at the clock on her dashboard – 4 a.m. She was embarrassed but wise enough to know that she had little choice but to seek the mercy of strangers. It was an old adobe with multiple additions and surrounded by a hodge-podge of outbuildings of various age and quality. Nearby were two doublewide modular homes, and Anna suspected members of the extended family occupied them. An older, run-down singlewide looked less well kept, possibly abandoned. Anna had known Celia came from one of the old land-grant families. She had seen a family living compound like this before.

Anna watched as Celia parked and then walked toward Anna's truck. Once again, Anna rolled down her window just enough to hear and be heard.

"You can park beside my car. I have a key. We can stay in my old room tonight."

Anna was surprised at the wave of nausea she felt at that thought. "No! I'll stay in my truck."

"But why?" Celia asked.

A flash of anger gave color to Anna's cheeks. "Don't you get it? Do you really think I'd ever let you touch me again?" She shook her head, trying to clear the confusion. "Why did I follow you?" Anna started the truck and put the gear into reverse just as lights came on in the house and on the porch and an old woman stepped outside, dressed in a full-length cotton nightgown, a mop of silver grey hair surrounding a beautiful face mapped with wrinkles and lines. Anna paused. For all the world, the only thing she wanted in that moment was to be wrapped in the comforting embrace of the *abuela* she saw before her.

"*Hola, Madre,*" Celia called.

"And what trouble do you bring home with you this time, *Hita?*" A scowl marred the beauty of the old woman's face.

"I lost my job," Celia said. "And I have a friend in trouble too. We have no place to go."

"Lost your job! I had hoped – working for the woman some say is a prophet – that maybe..." Her words faded, the message unfinished. The old woman slowly descended the front steps and walked toward where Celia stood beside Anna's truck. "Let me see who is with you."

Slowly, Anna got out of her truck.

"Move into the light where I can see you," the old woman said.

Anna did as instructed. She could only stare at the ground, ashamed at what the wise old woman might see in her face. Anna heard the woman give a sharp intake of breath.

"*¡Dios mio!* You are the *companera* to the prophet."

Anna gave a shaky breath and forced herself to look at the woman. "I was."

The old woman put a hand to her mouth and tears teased in her eyes. She turned to Celia. "What have you done?" She demanded.

"Mama, I—"

The woman silenced her daughter with an abrupt gesture of her hand. "Not now. In the morning." She gestured toward the dilapidated singlewide. "You can stay in your uncle's old trailer."

"Please," Anna said. She looked around the compound. "Is there a place in the barn, some other place I could sleep, at least for a few hours?"

The woman stepped to within a few inches of Anna. She put a gentle finger under Anna's chin and raised her face so they could look eye-to-eye. "You do not wish to stay with my daughter?"

"No, I do not," Anna said, deep conviction in her voice.

The old woman nodded slowly, pausing. Decision showed on her face. "You can stay in the house. You need rest. We will talk in the light of day."

From one of the doublewides, there was the sound of a screen door slamming. For the first time, Anna noticed lights in that house as well and a man, dressed haphazardly in jeans and an untucked shirt. He walked toward them.

"You okay, Mama?" he asked as he walked. He stopped when he got near Celia. "Oh, it's you again."

"Love you too, Brother," Celia answered.

"Only when you want something," he responded.

"Manny, get the *mujer's* suitcase and take it in

the house. Your sister will stay in your Uncle Tito's old trailer. She knows the way."

"Is the water on?" Celia asked.

"I'll turn it on tomorrow," her brother answered.

"But I need it tonight."

"You'll manage," the mother responded.

The man, who sported the broad shoulders and muscular arms of a man who understood physical labor, looked Anna up and down. "Are you sure, Mama?"

The old woman looked closely into Anna's face once again. "Yes, *Hito*, I'm sure."

❧ ❧ ❧ ❧

Anna slept. She was exhausted at all possible levels, physical, mental, emotional, and even spiritual. There were no dreams. That was a blessing for no dream escaping her current subconscious could possibly be pleasant. The sun was high in the sky when her consciousness finally fought its way to the surface. She was startled when she first opened her eyes, staring at the unfamiliar ceiling of the adobe home. She rolled onto her side and reached habitually for the woman who should be there. She reached for Kidwell. That was when the reality of the previous night hit her full force. Anna remembered, and she nearly strangled on a cry so primal that she was afraid the world would hear. She lay for a long time, without the will nor strength to move. She barely noticed the simple comfort of the room where she rested. The bedclothes and cover were old but clean and comfortable. A *niché* on the wall held a figure of Our Lady of Guadalupe, and a rosary was on the nightstand beside her. Anna had a vague memory of someone entering the room and leaving something on that nightstand. She felt certain that Celia's mother had included a prayer with that rosary, one that Anna desperately appreciated.

The door opened slightly; the *abuela* peeked through the crack and opened the door completely when she saw that Anna's eyes were open. She stepped inside the room, walking the slow but sure gait of a proud woman slowed by the arthritis of age. She took a seat on an antique, harped-back chair near the bed.

"Finally, you're awake," the woman said.

Anna pulled herself to a seat, leaning against the headboard. "I cannot tell you how grateful I am for you letting me stay here and to sleep so late."

"You needed rest and maybe some healing."

"Yes, I did," Anna answered.

"Still do?"

A tear slipped down Anna's cheek and she closed her eyes, fighting the flood of others that wanted to follow. "I don't think this wound will ever heal."

"My daughter, she did something bad?" the woman asked.

"*We* did something bad," Anna answered.

"I love my youngest, but I know her and what she has become. I see your heart. She took you where you did not want to go."

Anna wiped her eyes on the sleeve of her pajamas. The simple act brought a new wave of pain. She remembered that Kidwell's hands had packed those pajamas. Even hurt and angry, Kidwell had chosen her favorites to send with her.

"She may have led the way, but I made my own choices, bad as they were," Anna said.

"Do you wish to make it right?" the woman asked. She reached for a box of tissues on the dresser and handed it to Anna.

"With all my heart."

"Then do it."

Anna laughed a ragged, humorless laugh. "It's not that easy." Anna shook her head, trying to clarify her thoughts. "I think leaving may be what I must do to make it right. I am not strong enough to be what Kidwell needs. That makes me a burden."

"So, you give up?"

"What do you mean?" Anna asked.

The woman looked at Anna, her head tilted to one side, thinking. "When I was a child, we all lived off this land. There were no jobs, and for us all to have enough to eat and wood to heat our home through the winter, we had to work." A slow smile crossed her face as she remembered. "I remember when I was small, doing the simple jobs of a child – weeding the garden, shelling peas, picking *capulins*, helping Mamma to draw the water – sometimes I would tell my Papa that I was not strong enough. He would gently touch my head and say simply, then you must become stronger."

Anna felt the tears drying on her cheek. For a moment, she felt a flash of something she thought she'd never feel again – hope.

"What are you saying?" Anna asked.

"For a time at least, you can stay here. Maybe you will grow stronger."

"How?"

The old woman laughed. She took the rosary from the nightstand and placed it gently in Anna's hand. "I am not the one who can answer that question for you." She stood stiffly. "Now, you must dress. I'm sure you are hungry, and if you are to stay here, you must help with the work."

Celia knew her way around the old trailer. Since she'd first discovered the joy of alcohol and sex in her teen years, she had been banished to the trailer more than she'd lived in the house with her parents. That hadn't changed after her father's death from pneumonia, the price of being caught in a blizzard while feeding cattle. She had hoped her mother's soft heart would welcome her back, but no such luck. The trailer had been her bachelor uncle's for many years, but he was long dead, taken by a heart attack on a hot day while stacking hay nearly ten years earlier. It was too dark, and she was too tired to find the outside breaker box to turn on the electricity. The same was true of the shut off water line. She found a flashlight near the back door, and a canteen that had always hung in the mudroom. After filling it from an outside hydrant beside her brother's house, she peed in the dark woods beside the trailer and went inside.

Her own feelings confused Celia. The high of conquest disappeared mysteriously as she watched Kidwell wave her hand back at her apartment above the barn. There was an emptiness that she hadn't known for a long time, even a sense of shame that she had rarely felt. Celia sought comfort as she had so often before. She went to the bedroom and pulled out a dresser drawer, reaching behind to find her stash. She pulled out two plastic bags, one filled with green buds that also held a small, stone pipe, and a second with white powder. She debated a choice before deciding that she was too exhausted for the adrenaline of the cocaine and opted instead to smoke a bud. A few good puffs and she felt the tension, even the unfamiliar shame, start to evaporate. She drank deeply from the canteen, kicked off her boots, and curled on the bed, still clothed. She was asleep almost immediately. The glowing red in the marijuana faded quickly after she set the pipe on the dresser. There were already dark heat stains on the finish of the wood. She'd done this before. She slept deeply, not noticing the dark and somewhat rancid smell that started to fill the room. Even awake, she wouldn't have noticed the dark shadows moving of their own accord nor would she have heard their voiceless conversation.

"He's left her," the small one said. The soundless voice was high and piercing for any mind able to hear it.

"Fuck the light. It's the Enemy. She banished him, him so long saddled with this puny human," a darker, deeper voice responded.

"Did his job, he did," the small one said. The vibration of the dirty shape was intense and scattered.

"And now he's gone, the job half done," the deep voice said. The unpleasant smell increased with his anger. He turned glowing eyes toward the smaller form. "Someone must take his place."

"No, please," the little one said. "Want free, not tied to a human. No, master."

The dark figure growled and grew in size, making the smaller one vibrate at an even higher frequency in his fear. The small one rushed toward the sleeping woman and the merger was immediate. After all, she'd given permission so many times before. Celia stirred and moaned in her sleep. There was a familiar sense of filth in her heart, but she sighed in her sleep, no longer feeling alone.

Chapter Fourteen

First Flight

Kidwell felt time differently. Her mind still belonged to the woman she was before slipping through the dragon eye portal, but every day she remembered more and more of what it meant to be dragon. The passing of a day, a year, a century had different meaning for a species with lifespans over millennia. While it made a century relatively unimportant, oddly, it made each moment more precious. Kidwell knew there was time to savor the taste of a particularly juicy piece of meat. Time to enjoy a warm bath or listen to the rumbling purr of her niece when Kidwell woke in the night to realize that, once again, the young dragon had chosen a bed on the floor just to be near the aunt she so worshipped. She accepted the irrelevance of time and no longer worried about the return journey, about Aisha, Greg, and Martin. When she was ready, Kidwell would return with a heart far more at peace – not healed but at peace. She trusted her sister's assurance that she could choose the moment for her return, if it was after her departure. Her human friends would not worry, for they would never know that she'd been gone. She could take all the time she needed to process, to feel, to grieve.

In many ways, it was just another morning in this new dragon world she had once known so well. Still, since her return, there was an oddness to it, something missing. Over time, Kidwell identified the difference between her memories and this new dragon existence. She remembered people, the human allies who were riders, in many ways partners closer than any dragon could know with a fellow dragon friend, family, or mate. When human and dragon minds locked, there grew a symphony of motion between dragon and rider; there was a joining where it was as though they were one creature. There had never been many such pairs. It was rare for both dragons and humans to share the gift that made the merger possible. Even with the gift, many dragons chose not to join with a rider, for to do so was to embrace grief, to know well in advance of the agony to come. Yes, merger with a dragon prolonged human life, but the frail bodies of a human could not withstand the millennia granted a dragon existence. To take a rider was to know that, one day, a dragon would lose a piece of its soul with the passing of its human. If they were lucky, a few, a very few, of those blessed dragons would find the soul of their rider again, reincarnated in a different body. Because it happened, even rarely, it was a source of hope for those who lived with grief. Kidwell, known then by her dragon name, Harrana, did not intend to court such pain.

In a half-waking state, Kidwell remembered finding Annalome. Kidwell – Harrana, then – was still a young dragon, barely two centuries out of the shell when she swooped to capture a deer she spotted for her dinner, only to have an arrow strike the old buck before Kidwell could claim her meal. Annalome's arrow claimed venison to feed the people of her village, and so dragon and woman argued in a high mountain valley, each claiming the downed deer. A deal was struck. The woman's arrow had claimed the prey, but the young dragon would transport the weighty deer back to the village, claiming a full hindquarter in return. Fate intervened when they touched hands to seal the bargain.

Dragon finding rider and rider dragon had little to do with choice. It was all about frequency and vibration, compatibility of their very souls. Their briefest touch sent a ripple of vibration, not just through each of them but into the air and the earth around them. It was a bargain struck by the gods and goddesses, a contract signed and sealed for them, by them, but with no more consent other than a heart consumed by true love.

Kidwell lie on her dragon bed, smiling sweetly at the refreshed memory of that moment of joining with Annalome. Whether intended or not, it meant that they, as a pair, were now among the protectors of dragon and humankind alike. Kidwell stayed in the village for that evening meal as Annalome feasted with her people. There were dances of joy and tears of sorrow as her people said goodbye to Annalome. The people of the village knew what it meant when one of their own joined with a dragon. The night was still young when the escorts arrived, two pairs of seasoned dragons and riders. They had felt the vibration of the joining of two new sisters when Kidwell and Annalome touched. Together, the new dragon/rider pair left the village, following their escorts, their teachers, to the Weyr of Guardians. It would be their home until, until – Kidwell's memory could not go there. Not yet.

Kidwell's euphoria disappeared in an instant. The memory stopped, like a plug pulled on a projector. She rose and sat on the edge of the dragon bed, tendrils of distressed smoke seeping from her nostrils. All Kidwell knew was that there was a memory yet to come, one she did not wish to face.

A knock on the great hall door brought her back to the present. Masat entered.

"You slept well, Sister?" she asked.

"Too well, it would seem," Kidwell answered. "My still mind helped me remember more than I wished."

Masat looked sadly at her sister. "I forget that the old stories are coming back to you with all the freshness of yesterday. Do you remember it all, yet?"

"No. There is still a darkness, and each time I get close, my mind and heart slam a door. Will you tell me what I do not remember, Masat?"

Masat curled like a cat in a comfortable position before Kidwell. She paused long in thought. "I think not, Sister. If you are to be told, that is not my decision to make. It is best if your own memories tell you what you need to know."

"It involves Anna, doesn't it?

A troubled expression furrowed her brow, and Masat closed her eyes against a memory, still unpleasant despite millennium of healing. "Yes."

"Why does Maolan hate her so?" Kidwell asked.

"Again, Sister, it is best if your own memories take you on this journey without help from me."

Kidwell rumbled an expression of both frustration and determination. "Well, I can't wait forever for memories to come. I need some air."

Masat laughed. "Good to hear. It is a fine day. Come."

Masat led the way down the main corridor and out the front entrance. A large stone shelf overlooked the deep chasm and below to the valley far beneath. Kidwell gazed at the large squares of farmland along the alluvial basin in the valley below. She remembered fondly the earth dragons, not that much bigger than a large human, who lived a happy existence tending the land and water. There were vague memories of dear friends among their kind, and Kidwell decided that, in time, she hoped to find them.

Kidwell had already learned the joy of the cat-like curl of a dragon comfortably at rest. The two dragons curled close to one another, watching the activity of the weyr as their neighbors flew from place to place, home to home, or to the massive storage caverns that they all relied upon for food and other supplies. A very large dragon, fully loaded with large bags of produce and goods from the valley below, flew slowly to one such cavern. As she watched, Kidwell felt more than saw an interaction of magnetic forces wavering all around her. The sense triggered a different kind of memory, a body memory. She felt a calling in the air around her.

For the first time since her return, she watched the working dragons. Now that her healing had begun, Kidwell wondered how much of a burden she had been to family and weyr. It was not a pleasant thought.

"Sometime soon, I'd best find a way to earn my keep," Kidwell said.

Masat's voice had a sad note as she answered. "No one begrudges your place here, Harrana," she answered, using her sister's dragon name. "You were, still are a Guardian and you have paid a dear price to protect us all."

"Have I?" Kidwell asked. "I wish that I remembered what role I've played."

Masat placed a hand over her sister's. "If that is

what is best, you will get your wish."

Kidwell looked at their joined hands, noting the difference. Masat's were larger, stronger, and more birdlike. Kidwell's were more delicate, almost human in appearance except for the substantial claws and a leathery skin.

"Sister, why are we so different?" Kidwell asked.

"You already know that your egg was rescued by our mother, only a century before she departed to the golden realm."

"That I know, but it's not just like I'm from another family." Kidwell motioned toward the dragons flying around them. "I'm not like any of the other dragons."

"Of course not. You're one of the last of the ancient dragons of the East, after the great battles there with the demons and their human minions. The elder of your race, Meekian, brought your egg to us, entrusting Mother, the eldest of our race, to see to your hatching."

The dragons turned toward the entrance to their home when they heard a rustling. Allana appeared out of the darkness and curled up in a spot between her mother and aunt, carefully ensuring she could touch both her relatives.

"You came outside without me," Allana accused.

"My apologies, young one. I did not wish to disturb your studies."

Allana tried to look at her mother with disdain, but her purr negated the effect.

"Welcome, sweet niece." Kidwell smiled, but continued the conversation with her sister. "Meekian," Kidwell said. She remembered no face, no feature, but the name brought such peace to her. "I wish that I could speak with him, gain his guidance."

"But you can."

"What?" Kidwell responded. "He must be the ancient of the ancients. Surely he has passed to the golden realm."

Masat laughed. "Why do you think Allana so adores you? It is the tales told by Meekian that so entranced her when she was barely a hatchling. She is so proud to have one of the elder race in our very family."

"I can speak with him?" Kidwell asked.

"He would like nothing more. He has waited for you, dear Sister, but first, you must remember how to fly. It is a far journey to his solitary weyr."

Kidwell's deeper purr added harmony to her niece's. She looked to the sky around her, seeing and feeling more clearly the magnetic pull. It was everywhere, any direction she may wish.

"So, I must fly," Kidwell said.

"In due time, dear Sister," Masat responded.

"In due time," Kidwell responded. She jumped and leapt so quickly neither of the other dragons had a clue what was to come. Kidwell flew, catching the currents of magnetism, leaving her body memories totally in control.

"Hey!" Allana called, leaping after her aunt, and swooping in flight, using her wings, unaware of the magnetic pull that carried her aunt.

Masat laughed in joy and leapt as well so that the trio danced in flight. As an eastern dragon flew between the peaks and along the valley, all in the weyr watched. Like a wave, a roar of joy echoed, joined in time by the earth dragons far below as they looked to see the flight of a magic dragon.

The cacophony of activity caused Herber, the largest of the weyr's cargo dragons, to step to the entrance of the storage cavern where he had just delivered his load of produce from the valley below. Even his staid and steady heart beat in joy at the sight of the Eastern dragon flying in their very weyr. *Perhaps the prophecies are true,* he thought. He roared in joy with the rest of his dragon community, then he returned to the cavern to finish sorting his load. Prophecies or not, dragons still had to eat.

Chapter Fifteen

Dark Council

Screams echoed through the caverns. In the village above, people moaned in their sleep, twisted in beleaguered covers from their tossing and turning. Their ears did not hear the torment below, but their spirits felt the evil beneath. The presence they felt but never knew existed in the caverns far below had long cursed their land. It was there that demons took physical form and held counsel of war in a millennia-old effort to dominate and control the humans entrusted with care of this precarious planet.

Torment had begun for the failed demon. His punishment would not end any time soon, but it would continue elsewhere. When the portal opened, Celia's long-time possessor would be sent home in shame, a failure in a key mission.

The governor warmed himself near the magma river that lit and heated their deep-earth haven. These councils were precious to him, a rare time when they could all resonate in harmony with their adopted home and take physical form, live for a brief time as they had before entering the portal, invading this new planet, fulfilling the never-ending lust to perpetuate their essence, their darkness. For over ten thousand years, he had been cursed to live a half-existence, resonating so that he was never seen, only felt, choosing to live wherever life was darkest. He relished those times of true happiness for him when blood flowed in the streets of Jerusalem during the Crusades, and he never felt happier than hovering in the ovens and gas chambers of the Holocaust.

They must control humanity, or they must destroy them. That was their mission. They had come so close in the war to end all wars, only for the humanity they had assumed defeated to thwart them. More recently, he had been surprised, blind-sided by the Matrix – the legions of humans who had evolved to a new spiritual level, joining with the nuisance of light beings who aided them. Together, they created a web of light that simply made impossible the destruction of war he and his demons had worked so long and hard to weave.

As the frustrated governor gnashed his teeth, real physical teeth for once, his lower tusk pierced his upper lip and he sucked greedily at the dark blood, enjoying the pain of his injury.

"What say you, husband?" A grating voice interrupted his thoughts.

The governor turned to face his female counterpart, the governess.

"Dare you interrupt me?"

"Dare you deny me? I am not your minion."

The governor spat blood onto the edge of the magma river, listening with pleasure to the hiss as the blood evaporated on the super-heated rock.

He laughed without humor. "No, you are not. We share this burden of rule."

"The council is here," she said.

"And the torture of the failed minion, the one who was to destroy the Light One?"

The governess rubbed at her triple chin, careful

to enjoy the touch of a fresh oozing wound. "Can you not hear the screams?"

"When he enters the portal to our home, they must know that we prepared him adequately for his eternal punishment."

"Be assured, husband, the job is done." She hummed unpleasantly. "I do not wish to join him in that torment any more than you."

He turned to face the governess. For a moment, he felt a pang of regret. She had been human once, and beautiful. The darkness of her soul made her physical beauty lovelier. They needed a human to share in this rule, someone whose corrupted soul could lead them as they sought to corrupt others. No human beauty remained. Only in memory could he go back to the pleasures of their joining.

"The council awaits," she hissed.

The governor left the small hall beside the magma river and stepped into the echoing space of the council chambers. He strode past the rows of minion elders, a combination of demons from his original world and the collection of human souls corrupted in their millennial effort at conquest. These were the captains, those who nurtured pockets of evil throughout the world. The governor failed to acknowledge the empty spaces, those many who had failed and simply faded from existence or were sent by his own hand through the portal for eternal punishment. They had been strong not long ago, as strong as ever. That was before the Matrix, before the power of the Light Ones, the prophets that threatened their once-growing hold on the souls of humanity.

There was a cacophony of shrieks and calls and stones and sticks beaten on the cavern floor and walls as he entered. The minion captains acknowledged their leader.

"We banish a failure today," the governor called.

Cries for blood and punishment echoed from the crowd. It was expected.

"And we must decide how to regain our control, how to tighten our hold once again on humanity," the governor called. The room silenced. He scanned the faces. "How do we defeat the Light?"

"Kill the Light Ones," a weak voice said from the back.

"Discredit them, even better," another said, a captain near the front, still a hint of humanity to his appearance.

The governor nodded approval at this captain, a dark soul who still sported the tiny mustache, a family tradition, of which he had been so proud when a living person. This dark soul had been the governor's greatest success to date. He had been welcomed happily to the council.

"Adolph is right," the governor said. "Death without discredit only strengthens the Light in their followers."

"We must wait and watch," Adolph said, emboldened by the governor's praise. "The opportunity will come."

"Yes," the governor said. "Wait and watch. All of you must be our spies."

The council ended as the portal opened from his home world. A gaping black hole appeared in the air above them.

"Bring the prisoner," the governor called.

Two huge gargoyle-like guards dragged a skinless creature from a side tunnel. The failed demon had been returned to full physical form so that every nerve in his being could be exposed. Every touch was agony even greater than the fear and shame of his failure.

As they all looked above, they could see the faces of demons from the home world. No new demons could enter the human world, not since the magical closing during the great battle, although sometimes portals were opened to carry those already crossed from place-to-place. Only a willing and living human could open that portal, just as his governess and Adolph had done.

But demons could be returned, but the rules of the King would open that route only for those returned in shame and punishment until such a day that ultimate victory opened the portal. It was a day for which the governor had longed for ten thousand years.

The governor himself strode across the cavern, grasping the disgraced demon as roughly as possible, enhancing the agony. More than four times this minion's size, with little effort, the governor flung the disgraced servant toward the portal. The screams were silenced as the minion passed through the veil, and the portal snapped closed, leaving behind the stench of sulfur.

The cavern was silent.

"Go," the governor said. "I'm sickened by the sight of all of you."

There was a hum as all changed resonance, leaving the physical existence for that half existence of there but not there, returning to their posts throughout the world.

"Come, husband," the governess said. "I have prepared a meal of meat and bread for us to enjoy while we can."

The governor turned to his co-ruler. For just a moment, he thought he saw the golden tresses of her hair as she had once had.

Chapter Sixteen

Remembering

Kidwell purred and laughed at the antics of her niece as the younger dragon wove between them all, barely able to contain her excitement. Masat resorted solely to mind-to-mind instructions to her sister, unable to carry on a spoken conversation for the attention demanded of them both by the young dragon.

"I'm a strong flier. I could go with you," Allana insisted repeatedly until Masat glared at the younger dragon, puffs of irritated smoke drifting from the mother's nostrils.

Chastised, Allana finally halted her constant motion. She curled into a sullen pose at Kidwell's feet.

"This is not a journey for you, sweet niece," Kidwell said. For a moment, the light in her eyes dulled as her thoughts turned to the purpose for her coming journey. "I seek understanding for a deep darkness, young one, a darkness I pray you never need see." She glanced toward where Maolan waited patiently as the family said their farewells. "I need a guide who knows not only the way to the Eastern elder but who already knows the dark paths of the heart."

As their gazes met, Kidwell felt a deep kinship with Maolan. She still struggled to understand the bond she shared with the green dragon. It could not be defined, compartmentalized. Kidwell knew only her love for Anna could compare with the bond she felt for Maolan, perhaps because of the deep kinship from her flashes of memory when they had once been four, dragons and riders, the vanguard of Guardians for both worlds. The facts of the past were still a mystery to her, but she knew beyond a doubt here was a companion she could trust with her life, perhaps even her soul.

Maolan broke eye contact first, bowing her head slightly. "I am honored to be your guide on this journey," she said.

Kidwell stooped to touch her muzzle to her niece's forehead. "Precious child. You shall be the very first to hear my tales of this journey."

"Promise?" Allana asked.

"Promise," Kidwell answered with a deep chuckle. She stood tall, raising her long, Eastern dragon body above the heads of her dragon companions, almost like a snake writhing into the air. She nodded a farewell to her sister, an air of determination in her motion.

"Let's fly," Kidwell called, launching herself from the cliff edge, Maolan taking to the air an instant behind her. They circled once and then Maolan chose the direction, due to the East. Kidwell followed. Their journey had begun.

They flew together with speed, grace, and joy that Kidwell had not known for millennia, but felt as fresh to her as though it had been just as an instant. The leather straps of the pack she carried, filled with provisions for their two-day flight, precluded a need to hunt or forage. They flew with a speed that Kidwell only now remembered was possible. Rapidly, the weyr disappeared behind them and below was the wilderness of a world nearly empty of civilized communities, dragon or human. They rose higher in the air, high enough to limit the startled reaction of deer, bear, and the tiny beasts of the woods, and a thousand variety of birds caused by the passing of dragons.

If Kidwell let her mind fly as free as her body, she felt not a pack but a saddle, her rider, Annalome, seated there. Her senses quested for something that no longer existed for her – the deep bond between dragon and rider – but the memory was so intense that she knew its joy. The flight felt so familiar, even more so with the companion at her side; Maolan's spirit felt familiar too. Kidwell flew momentarily blind as she closed her eyes, letting her body memory take her back thousands of years when she flew not only with her rider but also with the pair who were their dearest companions. So real was the memory that she saw in her mind the clear image of a magnificent dragon, purple of hue and stronger than any other. She saw a brief glimpse of the woman who rode him, flashing green eyes and flowing auburn hair, glorious and confident in the flight, clothed in leather armor and the glean of sword and spear. So real was the memory that when Kidwell bellowed in joy and opened her eyes, she turned, expecting to see the memory rather than the glint of the sun on green from Maolan's shining scales.

The shock was so great that Kidwell momentarily lost control. She spiraled toward the ground, and Maolan trumpeted in distress, diving to Kidwell's side. She helped to steady her friend until Kidwell was once again in controlled flight. They slowed and drifted together to a grassy meadow beside a flowing river, deep woods of live oaks surrounding them.

Kidwell felt a confusion and distress that nearly consumed her. She crouched and moved in a circle, like a dog striving to build a bed in the grass. She finally paused, burying her face in the cool, flowing water. She drank deeply, the sensations of cold and wetness helping to ground her in the present.

"Harrana," Maolan said, using Kidwell's ancient dragon name. A note of concern deepened her tone. "What is wrong, dear friend?"

Kidwell turned to face Maolan, and she shook her head, trying to make peace with the image of the beautiful, auburn haired woman her mind still saw juxtaposed over the emerald green dragon she now knew as Maolan.

"You were human," Kidwell said.

"Yes," Maolan responded.

A depth of unexplained grief clutched at Kidwell's heart. She closed her eyes and her mind saw again the glorious purple dragon, and she knew the depth of love she had felt for him.

"Falong!" Kidwell cried, the intensity of her dragon voice echoing along the river and the hills. Birds flew and deer crashed through the brush, startled by the sound. Great hot tears fell from Kidwell's eyes, hissing as they hit the ground below. "My brother," she cried.

Maolan's tears fell too. "Yes, he was the finest, the fastest, the bravest of all."

Kidwell shuffled toward Maolan. "You were his rider. We all loved each other." She laid her head on Maolan's shoulder. "He's gone! Gone!"

"Yes, dear friend," Maolan whispered. "As he died, when all fell and the worlds split, I stayed with him and you with Annalome."

"So, you became dragon and I became human."

Maolan looked deeply into her companion's eyes.

There was a long pause. Kidwell watched the story told in Maolan's face. The emerald dragon struggled, wondering how much to say.

"The prophesies say that our choices, yours and mine, will matter to us all."

"What do you mean?"

Maolan, usually confident, shuffled from one foot to the other, undecided. "Meekian will know how to help you find the answers."

Kidwell lay full-length in the grass. She placed her head between her hands, taking a moment to collect herself.

"Yes, Meekian will have the answers," Kidwell said. She stood with a new confidence. "Let us continue our journey."

"Are you fit to fly?" Maolan asked.

In answer, Kidwell chuckled and launched herself into the air. Maolan followed. Together, they flew to the East. They flew for hours. For the first time since her return to dragon form, Kidwell flew beyond the joy of flight and knew the weariness that came with a long journey. She dropped to a position behind Maolan, content with direct flight, focusing on the destination rather than flight itself. As the sun lowered in the sky, Kidwell felt the magnetic connectivity that made her flight possible weaken, and it became difficult to maintain altitude and control.

Maolan, she thought, directing the call to her companion.

Yes, dear friend, came the answer.

I am weary.

As am I. Just a bit further, there is a way-place, a cave with a spring, Maolan added.

Kidwell had to slow her flight, concentrating to

make a controlled landing to where Maolan already waited. The cave was large, and a fire pit was blackened, placed below a natural chimney in the stone.

"Others have camped here," Kidwell said.

"Meekian does not share the location of his weyr with many, but there are those, leaders of the weyrs who sometimes seek his council. Many stop here for rest on their long journeys," Maolan responded.

They both dropped packs to the floor of the cavern. Maolan glanced toward the meager supply of firewood left by former campers. Then she returned to the entrance, looking over her shoulder to Kidwell.

"I'll return soon," she said. "We need more wood for the fire."

Kidwell busied herself, first stacking what wood was available and breathing a narrow stream of flame to start the fire. She then rummaged in the packs, laying out the huge haunches of dried venison, and full, ripe melons they had packed for the journey. She left out what they would need for that meal, placing the rest back in the packs. She did not bother to protect the remaining food from animals, as she always did as a human. Kidwell knew the smell of dragon was enough to deter even the largest bear. When Maolan returned, she had nearly the whole of two dead trees clasped, one in each clawed foot. Kidwell worked with her as they broke the wood into small pieces and stacked them just inside the entrance to the cave. They would have enough for the night and some to leave for the next traveler. They ate their meal hungrily, then built up the fire, quickly warming the chill of the cavern. After taking long drinks from the pool fed by a mountain spring at the back of the cave, they were both sated and weary. Their camp chores complete, they each returned to the ledge at the entrance, sharing, in companionable silence, the sight of a million stars blinking in the night sky and they watched together the rise of a golden half-moon.

"As much as I enjoy the mountains of my wilderness at home, I must say camping as a dragon is just as pleasurable," Kidwell said.

Maolan purred softly. *Perhaps it is the company*, she thought her answer.

Kidwell laughed with a hint of pain behind her humor. The companion with whom she had shared so many campfires was gone, perhaps forever. The twinge of pain did not overpower her pleasure in the moment.

Perhaps, Kidwell responded. *I'm tired. The flight today was magnificent, but I must sleep if we are to do it again tomorrow.*

Kidwell rose slowly and returned to the cavern, throwing more wood on the fire before choosing a spot near its warmth. She circled twice, like a dog making its nest, and then sunk to the floor, curling into a sleeping position. When Maolan followed, Kidwell did not move away when the green dragon lay close beside her. She even surprised herself as she found herself moving closer, enjoying the warmth of her companion, and relishing the feeling of love and safety.

❧ ❧ ❧ ❧

The feeling of *déjà vu* dizzied Kidwell. With Maolan leading, they had dropped altitude as they neared a craggy peak, all the mountains around taller and more imposing than those they'd left behind in the caves of the weyr of her family. The second day of the journey had been far shorter than the first, and, as they flew, the terrain felt more and more familiar to Kidwell. As they flew over a ridge, the feeling of familiarity became so strong that Kidwell circled abruptly, flying directly to a ridgeline that she remembered yet knew not at all. Maolan bellowed in surprise, alerted by changes in the sound of air interacting with Kidwell's flying form as the smaller dragon changed direction. Maolan pivoted neatly mid-air and followed Kidwell to a perch on a rocky outcropping.

"I thought you didn't remember," Maolan said as she folded her wings.

"I don't, but this feels so, well, 'right,'" Kidwell answered.

"We always paused here, gathering ourselves before meeting with the Ancient One."

"We?" Kidwell asked.

Maolan dipped her head, turning her gaze shyly away from Kidwell. "Perhaps I said too much."

Kidwell tilted her head to one side, looking deeply at her dragon companion. "I remember you, but it wasn't really you."

Maolan laughed. "It was me, all right. The universe changed all at once and with it, it changed me." She looked at Kidwell inquisitively. "And you."

"I became human?"

"Yes."

Kidwell held her breath and sat unmoving. The answer was almost there, teasing at the edge of her mind. Then it was gone, the almost memory slipping away like quicksilver. Smoke puffed from Kidwell's nostrils, and she growled in frustration.

Maolan laughed, but with little humor. "Meekian, you must see Meekian," she said.

"Yes," Kidwell answered.

With one powerful swoop of her wings, Maolan rose in the air. Kidwell followed, instinctively tapping into the line of electromagnetism that was her species' mode of flight. With certainty and skill, Maolan led the way, flying with precision through a chimney-like formation in the rocky slope, flying directly to the mouth of a cave, a rock ledge at its front, worn smooth by centuries of dragon comings and goings. They both landed neatly on the ledge.

"We are here," Maolan said.

Kidwell's *déjà vu* sensation solidified into more of a sensation of familiarity. She had a flash of memory of another dragon beside her, far larger and of a deeply magnificent purple color. *Falong*, Kidwell thought, knowing that she had a flash of memory of her long dead brother. She looked up to see Maolan staring at her, an odd expression causing her dragon eyes to reflect a rainbow of colors.

"What do you remember?" Maolan asked.

"My brother," Kidwell answered.

A gurgle of grief echoed quietly from Maolan's throat. "He was fine, as fine a dragon as ever took to the skies."

"You flew with him?"

Maolan laughed, more with frustration than humor. "Meekian," she said. "He will know how to answer."

"Perhaps I will," a voice said from within the darkness of the cavern entrance. A fine red, Chinese dragon stepped into the light of the late afternoon.

Maolan laughed, this time with real joy. "Master, it is so good to see you again. We miss your visits to our weyr. We miss the stories and the comfort of your wisdom."

"The centuries grow short these days, and I live in the comfort of my memories. Forgive me if I forget more and more to live in the present," the dragon answered.

He was half Maolan's size and somehow far grander than any other dragon Kidwell had seen. There was a slowness to his motion. It spoke of age, but in a way, unlike the humans Kidwell had known in their advanced years. Pain and uncertainty did not rule his motions. Kidwell suspected that having watched so much of the universe unfold over many millennium, connectivity to time itself slowed his movements.

Meekian, an ancient being among an ancient species, turned his full attention to Kidwell. She felt as if the ability to breathe left her body. Reflected in his eyes, she saw answers to questions she didn't yet know to ask.

"My dear, dear Harrana," he said, calling Kidwell by her dragon name. "You have finally come home."

He stepped close to her. Instinctively, Kidwell responded dipping her own head as they touched forehead to forehead. A wave of comfort filled her, and she felt a completeness to an absence she hadn't even realized was there.

"My daughter, my heir, the last of my own kind, welcome home."

They wept together. Joy or grief, Kidwell wasn't sure which. She only knew that the floodgates of something deep within her had opened. The tears of the two Chinese dragons – the grand ancient red and the confused and misplaced iridescent black – mixed, dropping to the stone of the ledge, pooling in a low depression. There was magic to those tears, the same for the music of the purring of the two dragons combined. The pool of mixed tears danced with a universe of colors, a rainbow beyond what any human eye could see or understand.

Meekian pulled ever so slightly away from the younger dragon.

"It is time," he whispered. "It is time for you to find your magic. It is time to remember. Look," he said. "Look into our tears."

As Kidwell opened her eyes and gazed into the shimmering pool, her mind transported to another time, perhaps the most critical time in all the universal layers of this world called Earth. A time where she and her companions had played such an important role.

※ ※ ※ ※

It was war! War like no one had ever imagined possible. Even the ancient Meekian could offer little comfort and expressed doubt in his own guidance. The veils between worlds of this universe were kept intentionally thin. Dragons and humans, unicorns and elves, felines, and so many more traveled freely between with common alliances. Occasional conflicts, even wars, posed no real threat to the balance of existence.

No one claimed responsibility, but it was a human, no doubt of that. Greed or curiosity had turned the freedom of the thinly veiled membranes into a threat to them all. A demon world, a dangerous world, an evil world had found its way to the existence of Earth, where humans bore the responsibility that came with sentience. Now dark forces walked the Earth freely and too many humans, vulnerable to the appeal of power and wealth, took that darkness to heart, becoming themselves not just allies but companions to the dark forces.

Harrana (for the name Kidwell would not be spoken for many centuries) flexed her body, still growing accustomed to the armor she wore. Annalome, her rider, the human half of her soul, stood beside her, holding hesitantly the humble staff that Meekian had entrusted to her and only her. They enjoyed quiet moments, filled with the anxiety of the great battle to come. Meekian, the ancient dragon, the wisest of the wise, had called for a secret pre-battle council for just four, two dragons and their riders.

"You and Harrana are our best hope," Meekian said gravely as he placed the plain cottonwood root staff in Annalome's hands. "The greatest magic and power all the elders could combine has been placed in the wood, but you must make actual contact with the breach in the veil between the demon world and human earth."

Harrana dipped her head over her rider's shoulder, looking closely at the simple wood. She sniffed, and her eyes opened wide. The staff looked and seemed simple. It would not appear any threat in the battle to come, but there was a strong smell of magic. It warmed Harrana's heart, and she began to purr spontaneously.

Meekian laughed. "Yes, Harrana. It is the embodiment of joy and peace and love that your rider shall use to close the breach, to save our worlds."

Annalome slid her hands gently over the smooth wood. "How do I wield such a weapon?" she asked.

"You do not carry a weapon," Meekian answered. "You carry a mighty talisman of healing. If you succeed, you will heal the rift, the tear bringing great evil to threaten us all. What demons may remain on this side will simply cease to exist."

"And if I fail?" Annalome asked, a quaver in her voice.

Meekian's gaze fell, and his lithe form huddled in despair. "Then we must close all the veils. Humanity will be left alone to deal with the contamination entering from the dark realm. The best magic we can offer as the veils close is to rob the demons of physical form. They can only continue their dark works through influence over their human minions."

"And dragons?" Harrana asked.

"Should that happen, dear Harrana, you must choose, to return to your home world or to remain with your rider, taking on human form and mortality."

"And what is our role?" asked the clear and strong voice of a woman from where she still sat atop her own dragon. The woman's striking auburn hair was gathered in a tight weave and hung below the metal of her war helmet. There was a lilt to her voice, a voice known in many halls for its beauty in song during more peaceful times. The dragon beneath her was massive, beautiful and of a purple hue that reflected iridescent light.

"Yes," the great dragon said. "What is our role?"

"Ah, Falong, your courage and strength will be sorely needed. You and Maolan are the greatest warriors of all the dragon-rider pairs. You shall be their protectors as Annalome and Harrana make for the breach."

Harrana gurgled a humorless laugh. "And we are not the greatest of the warrior pairs," she said.

Meekian laughed. "Our demon enemies only see strength in size and physical power. That is why it must be you two to carry the staff and create the healing. They do not know the talents of the dragons of the East. They do not know that in subtle ways, you have power no larger dragon can replicate. Harrana, when you are close enough to see clearly where you must go, you must teleport Annalome directly to the breach. She need only touch the staff to one piece of the edge." He turned his attention to Annalome. "Then it will be up to you."

"Are there words of magic I must say?" Annalome asked.

"You must simply believe, Annalome. Believe in love and light and goodness. Channel that through the staff, and the breach will close."

Drumbeats drifted to them where they held council on a high mountaintop. In the valley far below, an army marched – battalions of humans, felines, the magical equines of unicorns and winged horses. The drums and fifes of the humans kept beat with the marching feet. In the skies above, dragons and riders flew in formation, exploring ahead, and pausing to wait for the army they guarded. In the distance, the breach could be seen and below it a dark mass, like an anthill viewed from a distance. The armies of demons and dark humans awaited.

❧ ❧ ❧ ❧

Annalome's hands sweated on the hilt of the sword sheathed at her side. The magic staff was securely fastened to her back, readily available, but, hopefully, to be overlooked as they faced the enemy. She sat atop Harrana, and she valued the psychic strength her dragon now sent her way. The bond between them had been a part of her soul for so long that she couldn't remember how it had been to live without it. At that moment, it was strong, stronger than they had ever known. Her greatest comfort as she waited for the order to fly was that, come what may, she and Harrana would be together. She feared for her dragon far more than herself. If death were to come in battle, she prayed that it would be her or that they would die together. Annalome directed her own heart toward that of Harrana and the deep purr from the dragon felt as if it originated in her own chest. She heard the familiar duet of purrs as Falong, sitting close to their right, joined in heart-to-heart union with Maolan, his own rider. There were hundreds of purr-songs as many riders and dragons shared their own bonding as they waited, perched on the ridgelines above armies. The very earth reverberated with a purring symphony.

The armies faced each other, a green field between them, one that Annalome feared would soon turn red with blood. She could see Meekian in his battle position behind the armies, gathered in council with the various generals. One by one, those generals took to horse, riding to join their own armies. Soon only a handful of human, feline, and equine kings remained, Meekian staying to represent dragonkind.

The order came abruptly; war horns rang along the valley and on the hilltops above as the last of the generals arrived at his command. Annalome's heart lurched as Harrana bellowed, joining her dragon brothers and sisters in a great battle cry as they took to the air. Below, the allied armies marched in formation, heading toward the front line of demons. From the rear, great catapults launched stones and fiery bundles toward the demon armies. That would be the last notice Annalome would make of the marching armies. All attention was in the present as they met the first wave of demons mounted on winged pterodactyls or flying the viamanas they brought with them. Her leg below the knee was burned as a demon used some sort of flaming weapon as it flew to her right while she exchanged sword blows with a demon rider. Harrana changed direction slightly and ended the flame-throwing demon's days with a flash of her own fiery dragon breath. The beast screamed as he fell to the ground. His mount, only slightly burned, continued to fly toward the mountains, apparently grateful to be free of the unwelcome rider.

Closer, closer they came to the breach, a wide opening from the sky above to the earth below. Time and again, Falong and Maolan saved them, taking blows intended for the smaller dragon and rider, flying with great speed and Maolan firing deadly accurate arrows or wielding sword or spear. None escaped unscathed. Falong continued to fly, an arrow in his shoulder, hampering the movement of his right wing. Maolan risked leaving the security of the saddle to perch precariously on her dragon, drawing the arrow from his shoulder with a swift movement. She herself barely avoided a fatal arrow, dodging at the last minute, and suffering a deep cut to her cheek.

They fought and they fought, drawing ever closer to the breach. Annalome grew weary and the fear turned into a profound numbness. Harrana made maneuvers that surprised even Annalome, who thought she knew every trick of flight that her dragon could achieve. Annalome lost count of the heads and hands she severed as Harrana maneuvered her close to the enemy. Her once shiny shield was battered and the top had bent around her arm and over her hand.

Now, she heard in her mind Harrana's message.

Hold tight, now! the dragon commanded.

Annalome dropped the shield and sheathed her sword. She placed a hand on the staff to her back, clutching tightly to the saddle with her other hand. She felt the momentary dizziness of teleportation and then they were there, at the edge of the breach, at its highest point, as far from the earthbound arrows as Harrana could achieve. Annalome pulled the staff free and touched it to the edge of the breach.

Nothing happened.

Believe! Harrana called into Annalome's heart and mind. Annalome felt the love from her dragon and it began. She felt the love for humanity, for their universe and the staff seemed to come alive in her hand. It glowed brightly, and the breach began to close. Annalome barely spared a glance at what happened around them, but she was aware that Falong and Maolan, followed by three other dragon/rider pairs, had fought their way to them and were waging a great and brave battle against horrific odds to protect Annalome as she used the staff.

Victory was close, so close.

The spear was launched from below from some oversized bow or catapult. Harrana screamed in pain as it pierced her side, but she held position.

Fear filled Annalome and all love and hope disappeared. The staff went dark.

No, Annalome, no! Harrana screamed in her mind. *Hold true.*

Annalome tried again to connect with love and hope, but all she could feel was the pain of Harrana and the fear of losing her. The staff remained dark. Then she heard the deep scream of Falong; she looked in time to see him with a great spear protruding from his breast and he plunged toward the earth, his wings spread, fighting with his last breath to carry his rider safely to the ground.

The staff turned to dust in her hand. Harrana let out a cry of despair for all the universe to hear. Annalome felt the dizziness of teleportation and they were suddenly on the ground, landing hard, Annalome falling from the saddle. Harrana had carried them to be beside where Falong now lay; Maolan, bleeding from numerous wounds, knelt weeping beside him. Annalome pulled herself to be beside Harrana's head. She cradled the great head in her lap.

"Harrana," she cried, tears streaming through the filth of battle on her cheeks.

I shall live, Harrana thought to her. *Great gods help me, I shall live. My brother, my brother is gone.*

From over the shoulder of the fallen, great purple dragon, Maolan glared through eyes made greener by the depth of her tears. She looked with hatred at Annalome.

"You failed," she said. "My Falong died protecting you, and you failed."

Annalome struggled to breathe. She truly felt the weight of the universe on her shoulders, and she could not bear it.

The failure of Annalome and the staff triggered immediately the great magic the elders had prepared to provide what protection they could. What followed was a victory, of sorts. A three-note signal from allied horns throughout the battle sounded. In great hordes, those allies, both living and dead, of other worlds disappeared, retrieved back to their own realms.

I choose you, Harrana thought in her last words as a dragon. Annalome found herself kneeling not beside her wounded and beloved dragon but beside a woman, a stranger yet not strange, also wounded in the side as Harrana had been.

Annalome barely heard Maolan whisper as she lay across the fallen Falong. "I choose you," she said. Both fallen dragon and his beloved rider disappeared.

Yet still, the demons were robbed of their victory. As others were called home, the veils closed, the demons lost their physical form, and the breach faded and became transcendent, difficult to remain open.

Annalome lay beside the fallen woman, the former dragon, and wept. Despite her wounds, the woman moved to comfort Annalome.

"You did your best," she whispered. "It was a brave and risky enterprise. You tried. We tried."

Annalome roused herself from her grief. With all the strength she could muster, she bound the wounds of her companion.

❧❧❧❧

Kidwell lay despondent upon the stone shelf outside of Meekian's cave.

"You remember it all?" Maolan asked softly.

"Yes," Kidwell croaked; her voice was weak and sounded as full of despair as she felt. She lifted her head and looked directly at Maolan. "You were human."

"And you were dragon."

"In all the worlds, you are the only two who know what it's like to be both," Meekian said. He looked studiously at them both. "That may prove very important, but for now, Maolan, help me get Harrana inside the cave. She will need food and rest. Afterward, we must talk long of the past, the present, and the future."

Chapter Seventeen

Home Again

Allana would soon get her sleeping chamber to herself again. Most youth, dragon or human, would have been pleased to get their personal space back, but Kidwell knew her niece wasn't happy. The young dragon huddled near the doorway of the chamber.

Kidwell crossed to her young niece and curled to a sitting position beside her. Despite her disappointment and anger, the younger dragon soon leaned against her beloved aunt, and the rumble of a soft purr soon reverberated in her throat.

"Stay," Allana pleaded.

"I cannot, sweet child." Kidwell sighed so deeply that whiffs of smoke trickled from her nostrils. "Now that I remember, I know my purpose. Even as I begin to remember what it means to be dragon, my place, now at least, is with humanity. The struggle against evil continues and that is where I must be."

Maolan sat with stiff dignity. "Perhaps the child is wise," she said. "You have already given so much to save humans. You deserve a rest, a return to who you are."

Kidwell raised her head to gaze into the eyes of her friend. Her love for the dragon had grown since she remembered the times they had shared when Kidwell was dragon and Maolan her beloved brother's rider.

"You of all dragons should understand, Maolan. You were human once. The battle they fight affects us all."

The grand green dragon's eyes took on the rainbow glint of deep emotion. "And I have watched their foolishness for centuries. I am glad I chose dragon when the portals between worlds closed."

"Stop it! Both of you," Masat commanded.

"Whether we wanted it to be or not, we all knew from the moment my sister came home that she would return to her human life." She laughed. "Maolan, surely you did not think that Harrana – I'm sorry, Sister – I mean, Kidwell, would leave a job unfinished?"

"No, I did not," Maolan answered with a grudging grunt.

Kidwell walked to the swirling, eye-shaped opening in the cavern wall. It was the portal created by the dragon eye painting in her bedroom at the mountain cabin she had shared with Anna.

"Have you chosen the moment?" Masat asked.

Kidwell forced herself to look at the image through the eye. She saw her empty bedroom, the shape of her own human form still visible where she had lain crying just moments before. She had chosen a moment minutes from the time she had first fallen into the eye, unwittingly returning to a dragon existence she had not remembered for many human lifetimes.

"Yes," Kidwell answered. "I didn't want time to pass there, causing my friends to worry."

Masat stepped close to the smaller Chinese dragon who was her adopted sister. She lifted a wing and wrapped it warmly around Kidwell. "We shall watch from here, dear Sister. Remember the portal is open should you need to return."

Unnoticed, Allana had moved close and now inserted her head between her mother and aunt, making a space for herself. "Yes, you can return."

Kidwell laughed, touching forehead to forehead with her niece. *Wherever I am, you are in my heart, young one*, Kidwell answered through the intimacy of telepathy.

The chamber suddenly echoed with a great battle roar. Shocked, the other three dragons jumped to watchful attitudes and turned to Maolan, the source of the soul-tearing roar.

"You should not have to do this alone!" Maolan said loudly.

Kidwell stood close to her friend. "I have my human allies. They are not faint of heart."

Maolan looked at Kidwell with an openness rare for the dignified dragon warrior. She answered with thoughts intended for Kidwell alone.

Once we were four. I lost my heart, my soul to a spear when Falong fell. I lost Annalome to failure and betrayal. I lost you to the human world, and your return has eased the loneliness I had almost forgotten was there. Be safe, friend. Be safe. I need you.

And I you, dear Maolan. You and only you can best understand how I am torn between worlds. We shall be together again, dear friend. Only death could keep me from that promise, Kidwell answered.

A hot tear escaped from Maolan's eye, and it steamed as it hit the cold, stone floor. *That is what I fear. That is what I fear.*

Kidwell's dragon eyes reflected the rainbow colors of deep emotion. *I fully intend to stay alive and well.* She turned abruptly and lumbered in dragon haste to the eye portal.

Masat, blessed with the magic of temporal manipulation, muttered the magic words taught to her by Meekian. *Imagine the place and the time you choose,* she thought to Kidwell. Kidwell closed her eyes, recalling her room, willing the seconds after her departure.

"I love you all," she called. "I must go now while my determination is set."

She glanced one last time at the three dragons she loved so dearly, then she turned to the portal. Like quicksilver in a glass dish, her form flowed into something more light than solid and the ethereal shape slipped through the portal.

Kidwell fell to her knees as she took shape on the other side. She looked at her hands, seeing familiar human fingers that now felt odd and out of place.

"I'm back," she whispered to herself. She stood then and looked down at herself. She wore the same clothes she had on when she first slipped through the dragon-eye painting.

She stood unsteadily, taking a moment to adjust to the changes in balance and perspective going from dragon to human. *My friends. They are worried,* she thought, and she rushed from the room and down the stairs to the kitchen where she could hear Aisha, Greg, and Martin making the tiny comforting sounds of preparing a meal and talking in soft, concerned voices. All conversation ceased as she entered the kitchen. The three friends looked at her in surprise. Martin stood closest to her as he worked at the counter chopping onions. Kidwell moved to him, wrapping him in a bear hug.

"I'm back," she said, her voice muffled against

the flannel of his shirt.

"Back from where?" Aisha asked, sounding surprised and confused.

Instead of answering, Kidwell sniffed and then inhaled deeply.

"Coffee," she said. "How I've missed coffee."

"What in the hell are you talking about?" Greg demanded.

Kidwell took a cup from its hook beneath a cabinet and poured a fresh, hot cup of coffee from the pot.

"Sit down everyone. I have a very long story to tell," Kidwell answered.

Chapter Eighteen

Opportunity

I wish we could have ridden the horses," Aisha said as she adjusted the straps on her backpack.

Greg turned to his wife, the laughter in his voice mitigated by the tender expression in his eyes as he brushed a strand of her hair from her sweaty face. "I'm sorry, sweetheart. Maybe I could take some more of what's in your pack."

Aisha laughed. "You've already taken more than you should. Don't mind me. I've become soft." She paused and her expression gentled as she studied the trees and mountains surrounding her. "It's been too long since we've visited these woods, but I do miss having my little bay mare for company in these mountains."

Kidwell turned to her friends. "My apologies, dear Aisha, but I fear what I need to do would frighten the horses." She smiled. "Don't worry about your little mare. Martin is home, caring for all the horses and keeping the home fires burning."

Aisha looked long and hard at her fellow prophet. "Horses aren't the only ones. I think it may frighten me just a bit," she responded.

"Just a bit?" Greg asked. "We're about to see our best friend turn into a full-blown dragon." He placed a hand on Kidwell's shoulder. "No offense, Kidwell, but it is a bit, well, disconcerting."

"Disconcerting!" Kidwell responded. "When I first saw my own hand after being transformed, I tried to run from myself."

"That's an exercise in futility," Greg said.

"One that many of us try at some point in our lives," Aisha added.

Kidwell paused, thinking. "Yeah, you're right. Everyone tries, at some point at least, to run from those hidden dark places." She laughed. "Realizing I had secret claws, a snout, and the ability to breathe fire triggered a strong desire to run from myself, for a time at least."

"Breathe fire?" Aisha asked.

"Yes, not as well as some of the European dragons, but I can put out a little heat."

"Whoa!" Greg said. "Maybe I don't need to worry about wet firewood this trip."

Kidwell laughed. "We'll see."

The conversation stopped as they all began walking once again. For a time, the trail was steep, and breath was reserved for the effort of putting one foot in front of the other. Kidwell led, with Greg bringing up the rear, occasionally placing a hand under his wife's pack to help ease the load.

"Do you really think you can do this?" Aisha asked as the trail leveled and the effort required decreased.

"I hope so," Kidwell answered. "This is new territory. To my knowledge, there are only two who have ever been both dragon and human. If I can choose to be either in this world, there are so many possibilities. Also, Meekian, the ancient dragon who helped me, told me of things I can do as an Eastern dragon, things that the European dragons cannot. I have not tried them yet."

"Like what?" Greg asked.

Kidwell stopped, halting the march for them all. She looked around, as though wondering if she even dared let the trees hear what she had to say.

"Like being able to change my size, teleport, even change the frequency of my being to become invisible." She shook her head. She confounded even herself with what she'd just said. "It all seems unbelievable."

Aisha laughed. "Kidwell, what are you talking about? You and I have seen things beyond imagination. I have shared figs and fruit juice with The Prophet himself, and you have met and walked with the most powerful of magical beings. How can you find anything unbelievable?"

Kidwell smiled at her sister of spirit. "As usual, you are right, dear Aisha."

Greg looked down the trail as the two women talked. "While you two are planning how to save the universe, I'll take care of planning our campsite. If I'm not mistaken, there's a meadow with a spring ahead. It's the one where we camped the first night going up to Thunder Lake."

Both Kidwell and Aisha gazed to where he pointed. "I think you're right," Kidwell said.

"I think I'm lost," Aisha added. "But then I always am in the forest. I depend on you two to get me home."

Greg touched his wife's face. "Tonight, home will be our tent."

"If you are in it, then it is home," Aisha answered, a loving softness in her eyes as she looked at her husband.

Kidwell watched, feeling a stab of pain in her own heart. The joy for her friends was so intense it was almost pain, but seeing their love made her acutely aware at the grief she still felt at the absence of Anna, a pain she despaired of ever healing.

"Come on, you two. I'm hungry, and I want to get our camp set up before dark," Kidwell said.

It was a cheerful camp as they made ready their one-night home. Soon tents were set up, and a small campfire crackled, with a stone ring carefully placed. They would heat the water for freeze-dried meals and coffee with their pack stoves, but the small fire offered both comfort and the opportunity for companionship. When the meal was finished, they spread sleeping bags within the tents, the internal fibers expanding after compression in travel bags, increasing the insulation for warmth they would need in the cool mountain night.

"I'd forgotten how much I love a simple camping trip," Kidwell said. She held the warmth of her metal cup filled with instant cappuccino, as she lounged beside the fire. Greg and Aisha were cuddled comfortably on the far side of the fire, the gentle breeze carrying the smoke away in a path between them.

"It's good to see you relaxed and happy," Aisha said.

Kidwell stared at the liquid in her cup. For a time, the full memory and grief about Anna consumed her.

"Some pains never fully go away," Kidwell answered.

Greg tightened his arms around Aisha as she leaned against him, his own back resting against a small boulder. He buried his face in her hair. "I can't imagine what you must feel. To lose..." He held his wife tightly.

"It is what it is," Kidwell answered, taking

a cautious drink of the warm liquid. They sat in companionable silence. Kidwell finished her drink, poured a small amount of water from her water bottle into the cup, then walked to the edge of the camp, sloshing to rinse the cup as she walked before throwing the liquid into the woods. She approached the tree some distance from the camp to lower the bear bag from where it hung by a rope high in a tree some yards from the camp. All their edibles were inside the bag. She placed the cup, knowing that it still emanated the potentially bear attracting scent of the drink, inside the bag and then returned the bag to its high and safe position.

"Tomorrow's going to be a big day," Kidwell said as she walked back to the fire. "I'm going to hit the sleeping bag. Sleep well, dear friends."

"You too," Aisha said. Her head tilted to one side. "I wonder if I'll dream of dragons."

Kidwell smiled, the reflection from the fire giving the expression a new dimension. "If you do, just remember that they are friendly."

⁂

By the time Greg crawled out of their tent, Kidwell already had a real pot of coffee made, heated on the refreshed campfire. She loved that flavor, far better than the somewhat artificial taste of instant coffee. She shared Aisha's regret that they couldn't use the horses. Their weight bearing capacity truly improved camping comforts, but she was glad she had carried the small coffee pot in her pack.

"You're up early," Greg said.

"Excited," Kidwell answered. "I rather miss, well,

being a dragon."

"Did you sleep?"

"Like the dead for the first few hours. Our eight-mile hike yesterday wore me out, but I awoke excited before daylight."

"Hush you both," Aisha called from her tent. "Civilized people are still sleeping."

Greg laughed as he made for the woods to urinate in private. By the time Aisha exited the tent, a tad disheveled and still sleepy-eyed, Greg and Kidwell had prepared and eaten freeze-dried Mexican omelets, saving a generous share for Aisha.

"I don't understand how you both can sleep so well on the hard ground," Aisha said.

"We've had a little more practice," Greg answered.

Aisha had her sleeping bag wrapped around her shoulders as she sat beside the fire. Greg handed her a collapsible silicon plate filled with eggs along with a metal cup of coffee. Aisha drank the coffee greedily and nibbled at the eggs. When her stomach fully awoke, she progressed from nibbling to eating with relish.

"I did dream of dragons," she said, between bites.

"Were they friendly?" Kidwell asked.

"Of course, but terrifying too."

Kidwell looked at Aisha intently. "In what way?"

"There was this one that flew without wings. She took me for a ride. Allah help me, I've never been more terrified in a dream. I felt the ecstasy of flight and the terror of falling, all at the same time. It was horrible – and wonderful."

Kidwell knelt on one knee in front of her friend. "If all goes as hoped today, you may have the chance to experience that in real life." She touched Aisha's arm lightly. "I am a dragon that flies without wings."

"How?" Aisha asked.

A laugh was Kidwell's first answer. "I can't tell you the science. That's not part of the dragon world. I can only tell you the reality. I know that I can feel, well, attractions in all directions, and I can choose which to follow and the strength with which I follow those attractions." Kidwell sat on the ground, thinking. "I suppose it's something to do with the ability to manipulate electromagnetism."

"Fascinating," Greg said.

Kidwell pivoted to face the more scientific of her two friends. "Maybe, if Meekian was right about other abilities, that's how my species of dragon can manipulate size, location, and visibility as well."

Greg paced, thinking. "If you can tap into electromagnetic reality, there could be amazing abilities to manipulate space and physical materiality."

Aisha sighed. "I think I prefer the dragon reality. It just is what it is. We don't need to understand how everything works to simply enjoy that it does." She smiled at Greg. "Like the human heart. There is no science to love. Would you deny the reality of something so wonderful because it can't be explained by a scientist?"

Greg crossed to his wife. He stooped and gave her a kiss on the lips. "I'm a scientist. Not an idiot." He took her plate and cup and went to where the spring bubbled from a nearby rock, where he rinsed the dishes.

"Time to stop thinking and planning. Time to do something about it," Kidwell said. She stood and walked to the center of the meadow.

"What do you plan to do?" Greg asked.

"Not sure," Kidwell answered. "When I went through the portal, by accident, I automatically became dragon. If it is possible here, I guess I just need to, well, wish it."

"Trigger the electromagnetic manipulations?" Greg asked.

Aisha gave a loud hrumph. "Scientists," she said.

"Yeah," Kidwell responded. "Something like that."

She turned from her friends and stood in the meadow. Kidwell closed her eyes and wondered exactly how to proceed. She envisioned herself as a dragon, remembering her reflection in the bathing pool of her chamber. Nothing happened.

What do I do now? Kidwell wondered.

"Need help?" Greg asked.

"Any ideas?"

"What are you doing?"

"Trying to see myself as a dragon."

"Wrong approach," Aisha said.

"Why?" Kidwell asked.

"Don't try to see yourself. If you are to transform, you must *be* the dragon."

"Makes sense to me," Greg said.

Kidwell nodded agreement. She took a deep breath and then sat in a meditative position in the grass. She closed her eyes once again and tried to remember how it felt, sleeping with amazing comfort on cold stone. She remembered little things she never focused on consciously while a dragon. She felt the weight of her body, the fluidity of a body flexible at almost every vertebra. She recalled the constant and pleasant scent of her own breath, a hint of brimstone and fire. One moment she remembered. The next moment, she experienced the reality of that memory. She heard a sharp intake of breath from Aisha, then opened her eyes and she saw the world with the enhanced color spectrum of dragon eyes. She felt clearly the sensation of a magnetic world just as her human body knew the ever-present feel of the temperature of the surrounding air. Kidwell looked toward her companions and found herself gazing not across but down. Aisha and Greg stood staring upward, their mouths agape and their eyes wide.

"Good thing we left the horses," Greg said. "They'd be bolting into the woods."

"As would I if I didn't know it was you," Aisha said. Her face changed expression and Kidwell saw a depth in her old friend's eyes as Aisha looked upon a dragon with what Kidwell always thought of as her "artist's eye."

"What magnificent color," Aisha said. "You are black, but not. There is a shimmer of rainbow like the feathers on a raven in the sunlight."

Kidwell opened her mouth to speak. Although she thought in English, the words that came out were in dragon speak.

"Say what?" Greg asked.

I guess I can't yet speak any human language with my dragon tongue, Kidwell thought to her friends.

"I heard that, but in my mind," Aisha said.

"I heard it too," Greg answered.

Kidwell stretched, feeling joy she had not expected. She was dragon. She was her true self. She felt a roar welling inside her, and she did not try to contain it. The sound of songbird and crow caw died instantly as her roar echoed in the mountains. When the last of it faded away, the forest was silent. She looked to Greg and Aisha, and they stood, obviously shaken, their hands over their ears.

"That was impressive," Aisha said.

"And painful," Greg added, shaking his head.

Sorry, Kidwell thought to them. *Couldn't help myself.* She felt the magnetic pull around her and another uncontrollable urge almost overwhelmed her. *I must fly.* She turned to Aisha. *Want to come along?*

"I think I'll pass for now," Aisha said.

Kidwell launched herself into the air with ease. There seemed no difference from the flight she'd enjoyed in the dragon realm. *I can't be seen*, Kidwell thought, and then she felt an odd change in her being, a different vibration. When she looked down, she couldn't see her own clawed hand. *I guess invisibility is possible.*

That night they had a larger campfire. It was so easy to start with dragon fire.

Chapter Nineteen

Unseen

Hopelessly wrapped in the wadded sheets on her small bed, Anna struggled to be free. She fought with the fear of the nightmare, the recurring nightmare that came so many nights in the past few weeks. The sheets that bound her, wrapped and knotted from her tossing and turning as she struggled with the dream, added to the intensity of the fear and claustrophobia that followed her from the dream into the living world.

Finally, she kicked and struggled free and stepped to the window of the tiny room she had claimed as her own in the barn on the Martinez ancestral home. A breeze from the open window eased the heat of the dream, cooling the sweat soaking her thin nightshirt. The family had adopted her as one of their own, more welcome than Celia, the wayward daughter that they accepted because of blood but watched warily. Celia had left again. No one knew where. Except for an occasional sadness in Señora Martinez' eyes, no one seemed to care.

Anna was still welcome in the main house, accepted as a daughter, but she felt a need for simplicity, for solitude. When the dreams started, she found the disused tack room in the barn and asked to move there. She had expected little, but the sons and grandsons of

Señora Martinez had dropped everything, working for days to convert the room into a livable space.

"I don't deserve this," Anna said when they finally let her inside. The matriarch was applying finishing touches, gingham curtains at the window.

The old woman paused in her work, placing a hand on each side of Anna's face. "Heal, child. You made a bad mistake. You are not that mistake."

"Are you sure, *Abuela*?"

The elder looked deep into Anna's eyes. "You still have much to do. Find your wisdom. Find your strength." She looked around the tiny room, reminiscent of a nun's cell. "But when winter comes, you will return to the house."

"But I…"

The old woman turned stern. "You will return to the house. A frozen death brings wisdom to no one."

"Yes, *Abuela*," Anna answered.

Anna had settled into a routine on the Martinez Ranch. She worked hard, side-by-side with the sons, daughters, grandsons, granddaughters, and the *abuela* herself. They cared for the small herd of cows and calves, treated more like beloved pets than range animals. Goats provided meat, milk, cheese, and entertainment. For a time, Anna thought she'd forgotten how to laugh, but the dances of the kids reached beyond her grief and the sight gave her pleasure in the midst of pain. She picked chokecherries and worked side-by-side with the women in the arduous and backbreaking work of creating hundreds of jars of the family's famous chokecherry jelly. The work strengthened her body and eased her heart, giving her a purpose that kept the despair at bay. There were still intense moments of utter longing. At her first taste of the jelly she'd helped create, she remembered Kidwell's love of the local delicacy, and she left the house, finding a quiet place by a nearby creek where she sobbed, sobbed as though there were no tomorrow.

"My dearest, my Kidwell," Anna whispered to the night as she stood by the open window. She closed her eyes and imagined for an instant that the caress of the breeze against her sweat-damp skin was a gentle touch from Kidwell's cool fingers. "I miss you, my love."

That night, as she had done so many nights before, Anna looked into the night sky and tried to make sense of the dream, the dream that seemed so fantastic yet so real.

They flew, and Anna knew a joy and terror like no other. She held a staff in her right hand. Beneath her was a dragon, a grand dragon with the many colors of the rainbow so deep that, at a glance, she was indeed black. Love and fear for the dragon she rode consumed her entire being, her whole heart, but they had a task, a vital task. Anna held the key, the answer to save them all in the magic of the simple staff she held in her hand.

Chaos filled the air around them and the land below. Dragons and riders covered their flanks. She glanced at a magnificent purple dragon, ridden by a striking shield maiden, deep auburn hair and amazing skill with spear and bow. Love filled her again as she saw the pair. She knew them as brother and sister to herself and the dragon to whom she was completely bonded. The demons around them, mounted on winged reptiles or flying *viamanas* they had stolen from ancient peoples, put up a horrific battle. Their bonded siblings fought well; even as an arrow damaged the wing of the purple dragon, they flew on, his fiery breath downing beast and machine, and the shield maiden doing the same with arrows then spear and sword after the arrows were spent. The ground beneath them was cluttered with their conquests as they protected the flight of Anna and her dragon.

Anna and her dragon flew with purpose toward a terrific rent in the sky and land, a hole into another world where demons poured through, most terrible of invaders. Below them, humans, land dragons, unicorns, elves, magical peoples of all sorts battled against the flow of demons, striving to force them back to their hellish world.

They reached the rift, and Anna did as she knew she must. With all her mind and heart, she focused on love while she touched the staff to the edge of the tear in reality. There was a flash of light, and the opening began to close. She felt joy, hope. *Perhaps we will win*, she thought.

It was a massive wooden and iron bolt, fired from a hidden catapult in the brush below. Anna heard Harrana bellow from her wound and felt the pain as though it were her own. Despite injury, Harrana did not move from her position beside the rift.

"No!" Anna screamed.

Stay your arm. Hold, dearest, she heard in her mind. Anna felt her dragon will strength to her, striving to help keep the staff in contact with the horrid rift, already half closed.

Then the second bolt hit, just before another dragon found the catapult, spouting fire and turning it into cinders. Anna looked below in time to see Falong and Maolan as they fell to the ground, the fatally injured dragon struggling to fly, slowing their descent.

The bond between dragon and rider wove through the fiber of their beings. Anna felt the pain of the wound that now crippled her dragon. She weakened. With no realization of what she'd done, Anna's hand lost strength, the love she needed to work the spell faded, replaced by fear, and the staff slipped through her fingers.

No! Hold on! Her dragon screamed in her mind.

Too late. As the staff plunged to the earth, turning to dust as it fell, she and her dragon followed. So, too, did all their hopes.

❧❧❧❧

Anna wept as she stood by the window. Failed. She had failed them all.

Weary, she returned to her narrow bed. She straightened the sheets and sought comfort in the warmth of the mattress and the hand-made quilt the *abuela* had given her. She looked to the small painting framed on the wall near her bed. It was a simple scene; one Aisha had painted for her with a high peak in the distance and a small stream nearby. It had been among the things Kidwell had packed for her, and it had become her most precious possession.

The eyes of her soul had been closed. She did not see the gold figure sitting in the plain wooden chair beside the bed. As Anna wept, the angel leaned over her, watching as she had so many times before. A golden hand rested on Anna's head.

"Sleep, blessed one," the angel said, unheard by Anna's ears if not her heart. "There is still hope."

Anna sighed and fell into a deep sleep.

Chapter Twenty

Monster Trap

Roberto stared long and hard at the phone receiver in his hand before he finally returned it to its cradle. The conversation had been bizarre. He knew Kidwell. They met through the same Mother Superior who recruited Kidwell to help combat the drug warlord in the ancient Mayan lands. The inability to capture that drug lord was one of Roberto's greatest frustrations and failures in his work at the International Court of Justice. Through different extraditions, they would occasionally capture one of his lieutenants when they left the virtual kingdom of the drug baron's domain, but he never left, was never in a place where legitimate government or law enforcement had the power to arrest and extradite. As long as he lived and was free, the reign of terror and crime continued. Roberto followed the facts – the number of native citizens forced into slavery to work the poppy fields or the work sheds where the poppies became heroin, those killed by his army of minions. He'd secretly hoped the famous Kidwell Brown could make a difference, but his practical mind prepared him. He was not surprised when he learned of her failure.

They had become friends as he'd fed her what intelligence he had about the drug lord, his enforcers, and his holdings. She, in turn, had reported what she learned as she hid and worked in the villages of his domain, but he had never expected to hear from her again. It had been one of his greatest joys and surprises to learn that she had escaped, unharmed. He thought back on that conversation as he turned to his computer.

"*Hola,* Roberto," Kidwell said as he picked up the phone.

"Kidwell," he said, sincere joy in his voice. "It is so good to hear from you. Where are you? Tell me you are in the Netherlands. I wish to meet you in person."

"Well," Kidwell paused. "I'm still in New Mexico."

"Ah, then we will not meet very soon."

A silence so intense it nearly hurt his ears was his only answer. "Kidwell, are you still there?"

"Yes. Roberto, I don't know how to tell you this. You won't believe me, but we are going to meet very, very soon."

Roberto looked at the clock over his desk. "If you fly out today, you should arrive sometime tomorrow. Let me know when, and I'll pick you up at the airport."

"Do you believe in miracles, Roberto?"

He paused, thinking before he answered. He remembered the secret optimism when he heard that Kidwell Brown, a prophet some said, was going to his homeland.

"Yes," he answered.

"Then just have faith for a bit. You will understand soon, but I can't explain. You must see, but I need you to do me a favor."

"You only need to ask."

Kidwell laughed. "As closely as we worked together through phone and internet, I've never seen your face or even your office."

"That is true. I feel like I know you so hadn't

thought about that."

"I need you to email me a picture of either you or the room where you are right now."

"What?" Roberto was surprised.

"Please, just do it. Is anyone there with you?"

"No," he answered, puzzled. He could hear muffled voices from other offices down the hall. "There are others in the building, but not in my office."

"Can you close and lock the door?"

"Yes, but…"

"Please, Roberto. You must trust me. You will soon see a miracle, but you must not be frightened nor call out. This must be just between you and me."

Roberto felt his heart rate increase. "What?"

"Just send the picture, close and lock your door, and wait. It won't take long."

"Well, all right." Roberto could see no harm in emailing a picture to this woman whom he totally trusted.

"Bye for now, Roberto, but not for long."

"*Adios,*" he answered. He slowly hung up the phone and turned to his computer. It only took a few moments to snap a picture with the built-in camera. The photo showed him sitting at his desk, the office behind him. He attached the photo to an email, entered Kidwell's address, and hit send.

He rose to close and lock the door then sat staring at the computer, puzzled to the point of confusion. He laughed and tried to turn his attention to opening and answering emails, when he felt a strange sensation, as if someone was behind him. Roberto swiveled his chair in time to catch an image of a strange, dark outline, flickering with a hint of rainbows, then solidifying. Before him stood Kidwell Brown. This officer of the World Court, this man who thought he'd seen everything, was speechless.

"*Como*…how…what?"

"Teleportation is the simple word, Roberto. I've discovered I have hidden gifts."

"Obviously! But why here? Why to me?"

"The drug lord," Kidwell answered. "I intend to bring him to you."

Roberto looked at the slight woman before him. He remembered the intelligence reports of not only of the lord's constant bodyguard, but of his own obsession, vanity really, of maintaining his own fighting skills.

"Even if you can teleport there, how could you subdue him?"

Kidwell took a deep breath. "There's more, and this is the part you may find frightening."

"I can live with a little fear if it will protect people from that monster."

Taking two quick steps toward him, Kidwell firmly grasped his shoulder. "You must not call out, and remember, it is me. You have nothing to fear from what you see."

Roberto's rapid heart rate quickened further. "Do what you are here to do," he said.

Kidwell stepped back to the center of the room. He watched as her shape shimmered and changed, and his breath caught in his chest as a magnificent dragon appeared where Kidwell had stood. The dragon was dark, almost black except for the shimmer of rainbow across her body as she moved in the light.

I can adapt my size as well, he heard in his mind. *I have adjusted so that I will not destroy your office. Overpowering the drug lord will not be a problem.*

Her shape shimmered again. Once again, the

woman stood before him.

"When you arrest someone, where are they imprisoned while they await trial?" she asked.

"We have a small, well-guarded facility."

"Are there any guards whom you would trust with our secret?"

"Yes."

"Can you and I meet them there, preferably where you would like to have a prisoner arrive for processing?"

"When?" he asked.

"Now," Kidwell answered. She looked at the watch on her wrist. "It's 2 a.m. there. If we hurry, we can have him in custody within the hour."

"But we need to research, gain information, see the layout of his—"

"I was just there," Kidwell said. "All I had to do was envision the son-of-a-bitch, and I was there."

"But you could have been spotted, even killed."

Kidwell laughed. "I told you I had new gifts. I can will myself even smaller and unseen. He's sound asleep with no bodyguards nearby. We can do it now."

Tears pooled in Roberto's eyes. "The Mother Superior tells me that his goons have killed nine people this month."

"Then let's try to keep it from being ten," Kidwell said. "If we don't act soon, it will eventually be her."

Roberto pulled his cell phone from his pocket. He was already dialing the direct number of the guard whom he trusted most.

❧ ❧ ❧ ❧

Kidwell stood, stunned, alone for the first time in hours. Outside was the dark and cold of the depth of a

Dutch night. The damp crept through her clothes and down to her very bones, even in the environmentally controlled air of the building. She was a woman of the desert, feeling terribly foreign in this land that survived because the sea was kept at bay. Roberto had escorted her past the night guards before turning to stride back toward the small, high security prison. He wanted her to stay in The Hague or Amsterdam, to meet with some high-ranking official who must know their secrets if their plan was to work in bringing the world's worst criminals to justice. Outside, a car awaited her, a Dutch soldier as her driver, and Roberto had arranged a room at a nearby hotel. Kidwell wanted a hot meal and an even hotter shower, but she paused in the silence of the dimly lit hallway, lights low in the nearly empty building. It was the first silence she'd had to gather her thoughts.

I always did want to see The Hague, she thought, deciding in that moment to stay an extra day or two just to enjoy the Netherlands. Her passport was in her pocket, placed there before she first teleported to Roberto's office. She was certain he could arrange an explanation for why no entry stamp placed her in the country where she now stood.

The capture had gone off so smoothly that it didn't feel real. Kidwell, dragon and invisible, teleported to where the drug lord snored loudly, sprawled across his bed and still wearing his rumpled clothing. He smelled to high heaven of the tequila that induced his near comatose sleep. Kidwell gently clutched his right ankle in her left front paw. She closed her eyes and envisioned the holding cell where Roberto and two guards awaited. The drug lord never woke. The guards laughed as they lifted him to the cell's solitary bunk, taking time to remove his boots and belt and search his clothing, removing the contents of his pockets and ensuring he had no weapons. They spoke softly in Dutch, laughing quietly at the unconscious drunk. Kidwell found herself smiling at the idiocy of a man who instilled so much terror in his own domain, a terror he could not impose in the cell that was his new home.

Kidwell closed her eyes and took several deep breaths, gathering herself. When she opened her eyes again, she felt much more at peace, less disoriented. She pushed open the door and stepped outside.

The tropical heat surprised her momentarily, but as soon as she looked around, Kidwell knew exactly where she was. In the distance, she saw the stark white of a pyramid peeping over the canopy of the jungle. The warmth of mid-morning had replaced night.

"Welcome," a voice said.

Kidwell turned to consider the dark eyes of the Mayan goddess, Tonantzin. "I could not believe your brother when he said I could still help your people," Kidwell said.

"But you did not know who you truly were then," the goddess answered, stepping close to Kidwell.

They turned together, walking in companionable silence beside the rim of a deep cenote. Kidwell glanced over the edge, peering into the clear water, seeing the glint of gold deep within the waters. *Some gift left for the goddess,* Kidwell thought.

"Perhaps now my people can thrive again. with that snake brought to justice," Tonantzin said.

"I pray that is the case," Kidwell said.

The goddess placed a hand on Kidwell's arm, halting their walk and turning Kidwell to face her.

"The head of the snake may be gone, but beware the vipers that serve him," she warned.

It felt like a cold hand grasped her heart. "I shall try, goddess. I shall try."

They walked again, in silence. Kidwell felt the damp chill of the Netherlands fade from her bones, replaced by the damp warmth of the tropics. As they walked, Kidwell remembered Tonantzin's brother as she had first seen him, sitting on the Mayan throne as the great winged serpent, Quetzalcoatl.

Kidwell looked at Tonantzin in her feathered headdress and the white and gold of her garment. Kidwell knew that the feathers and clothing of her human form reflected the feathered wings and bright scales of her serpent form.

"I now know, I am dragon," Kidwell said.

"Yes, we have watched as you learned."

"Are we—" Kidwell hesitated. "—Are we related?"

Tonantzin laughed. "Very distantly, but, if you will allow it, I will proudly claim you as cousin."

Kidwell stopped short. "You would be proud? I, well, I feel too humble to claim that kinship."

The goddess placed a gentle hand on the side of Kidwell's face. "We should all be humble, dear friend. And we should all be proud. All the universe is connected." The goddess sighed. "The only real difference between us involves the choices we make. Right, cousin?"

Kidwell laughed. "Who am I to question the wisdom of a goddess?"

The goddess laughed in response. "Perhaps, and who am I to question the courage of one who chose mortality and the blindness of reincarnation to try to save us all?"

"I chose?"

The goddess laughed again, looping her arm through Kidwell's. "Enough of this deep conversation. You need food and rest." A door appeared before them in the jungle. It was a familiar door, the very one Kidwell had opened back in the Netherlands. "Go, the driver awaits. Just know that we are grateful, my brother and I."

"I am honored that you brought me here to tell me that," Kidwell responded.

The goddess waved her hand and the door opened magically. A gust of damp, cold air blew through. Tonantzin shivered. "I send you back to that cold place. I hope that knowing you are held warm in my heart will help you survive that far, northern land."

"It will," Kidwell said. She looked through the open door and could see the dark of a Dutch night. As she wrapped her jacket around her and stepped through the door, she hoped that she spoke the truth.

Chapter Twenty-one

Repercussions

Maolan bellowed in frustration. Allana, usually a fearless young dragon, slipped behind her mother. The child placed the older dragon between herself and the furious green dragon.

"We will find a way to get word to her," Masat said, containing her own fear and frustration as she leaned into her daughter, comforting the younger dragon.

Maolan looked to the pair, becoming aware of how she had frightened the child. She forced herself to sit, stopping her angry pacing. She took a deep breath to calm herself, but she could not contain the tendrils of smoke that puffed from her nostrils as she exhaled, her depth of emotion fanning the heat within her.

"Why did we not think to ensure we could communicate while she was in the human world?" Maolan said.

"As long as she was at her home, there was no problem," Masat said. "We had the magic dragon eye painted by Aisha."

"But she is not home."

"We know she was successful in capturing the villain," Masat said.

Allana danced around her mother. "I helped, or we wouldn't know."

Maolan's mood improved as she studied the excited youth. "Yes, you did, child. I would not have thought to seek the new paintings made by the sister prophet."

Masat barked a humorless laugh. "Thank the gods one family hung theirs in the meeting hall of their home."

"That magic box," Allana said. "I have learned so much watching."

Masat looked askance at her daughter. "Television, it's called, and what have you learned from made up stories and pretend magic?"

"But it looks so real," Allana said. "If only Dr. Who could fit me in his Tardis, I could go back to the great battle and stop it all. Uncle Falong would still be this side of the veil and Aunt Harrana would never have become human."

Maolan crossed to Allana and gently ran a clawed hand along the child's face. "I have a similar fantasy, dear child." She began to pace again, but the terrifying intensity of her fear and frustration was contained. "We must warn Harrana – Kidwell," she said.

"We will find a way," Masat said. "We know that she captured the villain. It was on the – what is it called? – the news on the magic box."

"We saw Harrana in her human form, but it was just a glimpse," Maolan said.

"It looked so cold there. She must be miserable," Allana said.

Masat returned to the window, the portal through which they could see other worlds where there were portals on the other side. "Cold and without a portal to be found in that city called The Hague."

"There was no mention of her on the magic box.

It is only luck that we caught a glimpse of her as they interviewed the dark-skinned man," Maolan said.

"His name was Roberto…something. He would not tell how the man was captured," Masat added.

Maolan laughed humorously. "I doubt the human world would understand or believe if he did tell them."

"But the magic box shows dragons," Allana said.

Her mother looked at her with a gentle smile. "Harrana explained that to you, sweet daughter. It's called special effects. The people know that the moving stories are not real."

"They look real, "Allana said.

"Most humans have lost touch with real magic, daughter. Instead, they can only create pretend magic."

Masat returned her attention to the portal and closed her eyes. She envisioned the receiving site she wished to access. It was far more ancient than any of Aisha's paintings. It was a serpent, chiseled into stone and stolen from a Mayan temple by the drug lord Kidwell had captured. Little did he know, when he placed it in the palace he'd created with his ill-gotten gains, that he was creating an opportunity for those in the dragon realm to spy on the very heart of his operation. The massive dining room where he'd had workers – little more than slaves – place the stone was the main meeting area when he called together his lieutenants and enforcers. Dragons needed no knowledge of Spanish to understand. They tapped directly into the thoughts of those there, an assortment of firearms always on the table before them. Truthfully, the dragons knew more than the drug lord, including how many of his minions prayed for a way to escape the life that entrapped them.

As they all looked through the portal, they saw

a room cast in darkness, peaceful even. There was no sign of the chaos of a few hours earlier, when one of the drug lord's lieutenants shot another, taking his place as head of the empire in the master's absence. The heated debate, the one that placed cold fear in the hearts of the dragon observers, was over, but they would not forget the outcome.

The drug army knew, or at least they'd convinced themselves, that Kidwell was behind the capture of their lord. The new commander had ripped the shirt from his fallen comrade and used it to wipe blood from the table's surface before spreading maps and papers across the table. They knew where Kidwell lived. They did not intend for her to live anywhere for much longer. The new leader selected six men to travel to New Mexico, six men to ensure the death of Kidwell Brown. Masat closed her eyes again, and the image in the portal shimmered and changed to the master bedroom at Kidwell's home, where the dragon eye painting hung.

"She's still not home," Maolan said. "Besides, if we warn her there, it may be too late."

Masat closed her eyes and the image shimmered again, this time to Aisha's painting studio. No one was there.

"Where could she be?" Maolan demanded.

"I don't know," Masat said, not for the first time since they'd learned of the danger to Kidwell. "We'll keep checking."

"There must be some other way to warn her," Maolan demanded.

Masat paused, her eyes closed, and her face tensed with thought. "There is one," she finally said.

Maolan stood tall, excited. "What?   Who?

Where?"

There was a look of caution on Masat's face as she turned to look directly at the green dragon. "Allana," she said over her shoulder, still looking at Maolan, "Go check on the meat roasting for dinner."

"It is in the pit. It will be hours yet," her daughter said.

Masat bent to look directly into her daughter's eyes. "Go."

"But—" Allana began.

"Go!" Masat commanded.

Grumbling, the young dragon exited the chamber.

"Only those who already know of our presence or those whom we have known one-on-one can hear our call through the portals," Masat said.

"I know that," Maolan answered, impatient.

"There is one with an Aisha painting. She has known you."

Maolan was puzzled. "When? I have known no living human except Kidwell."

"Yes, you have."

As realization dawned, smoke once again drifted from Maolan's nostrils. "No," she said.

"Is your hate for her stronger than your love for Harrana, for Kidwell?"

"I swore I would kill her should we ever meet again. Because of her, Falong died. Because of her, Harrana was exiled to the human world and me to here. Because of her, almost all was lost."

"And maybe, now, because of her, Harrana can be saved," Masat said.

"No!" Maolan called again. In agony, she dropped to a seat on her haunches and moaned softly.

"I can think of no other way to warn Harrana."

"No!"

"Maolan, please, find what measure of forgiveness you need," Masat said. She placed a hand beside Maolan's face, gently lowering the other dragon's head so she could look directly into her eyes. "Please, you are the only one who can save my sister."

A moan escaped Maolan's lips, one that proved her emotional pain was so profound it was physical. A hot tear slid down her cheek and fell, sizzling, to the stone floor.

"All right," Maolan said. She opened her eyes and looked to the portal. "I don't think I have the heart to call the image."

"I will call it," Masat said. "But she can only hear you."

Masat stood before the portal and closed her eyes. The image shimmered until, before them, they could see the darkened room of Anna Montoya. Anna herself lay sleeping, the portal just inches from her face.

Maolan took a deep breath. *Annalome, awake,* she thought, willing the message to the sleeping woman.

Anna stirred.

Annalome, Maolan thought, allowing a hint of her anger into the thought, hoping the intensity would rouse the sleeping woman.

Anna sat up abruptly, the covers falling away, showing her clothed in only a thin t-shirt.

"What?" Anna said in a frightened voice. "Who's there?"

Look to the painting, the painting Aisha made, Maolan thought.

Anna turned to her left and gasped as she saw the fluid image of an eye in place of the simple landscape that was in the painting. She pulled the cover up, covering her breasts barely hidden by the thin material of the shirt. She reached to the nightstand and turned on the light. On both sides of the portal, they blinked as their eyes adjusted to the light.

"Who are you? What do you want?" she demanded.

Maolan laughed derisively. *There is no need to cover yourself. It is most certainly not you that I want.*

"Then what?"

Harrana – Kidwell is in danger. You must warn her.

Maolan saw Anna's face go deathly white. "Kidwell, please God, no. Not Kidwell."

If you still care for her, you must act now.

"What can I do?"

Maolan closed her eyes and composed a rush of images and words, sending them in a hailstorm directly to Anna's mind. She told of the capture of the drug lord, of Kidwell's role, of the lord's lieutenant, and his plan to send men to New Mexico to assassinate Kidwell. By the time she was done, tears were streaming down both their faces, and Anna held her head, feeling an agony of pain from the unaccustomed flood of telepathy.

"No," Anna moaned. "When will they come?"

We don't know for certain. They may be on their way now.

"Where is Kidwell?"

We've lost touch. We think she is in that cold city, the one called The Hague.

"She worked with someone there when she went to Central America, someone named Roberto," Anna said.

Can you contact him?

Anna bit her lip, regretting the lack of access of Kidwell's contact list. "No," she answered. Her face brightened slightly. "But I know who I can call, Admiral O'Hare."

Who is that?

"Kidwell's old commander, and a dear friend and mentor. He'll believe me, and he has the connections to make the right people believe him," Anna answered.

Anna reached for her cell phone, then paused. She turned to the eye in the portal. The depth of the telepathic connection had told her more than the essential facts.

"You hate me," she said.

Maolan fumed. *Whether I do or I don't, you must warn Kidwell.*

"Why? Why do you hate me?" Anna asked.

That doesn't matter. Warn her!

The eye shimmered and faded away, leaving the original painting in its place. Anna looked to her phone, relieved that Admiral O'Hare's number was still in her contact list. She didn't even hesitate, thinking that she would wake the O'Hares from a deep sleep. As the phone rang, she had a puzzling realization. She had felt no surprise to learn that Kidwell had a dragon life. The dream almost made sense now. She heard the Admiral's sleepy voice before she had time to complete the thought.

⁂

Meekian stood on the stone ledge beside his cave, waiting for Maolan's arrival. She marveled that, no matter how many years, decades, even centuries between her visits, the elder dragon always knew when she would arrive. She glided to a landing beside the wise dragon.

"I need your guidance, Master," she said.

"I know. I have been watching."

"You know Harrana is in danger," Maolan said.

"And with her danger, we all face an uncertain future."

"What more can we do?" Maolan asked.

The old dragon smiled slyly. "Harrana walks in both worlds, for she has been both dragon and human."

"Yes, I understand that," Maolan said.

"She is not the only one," the dragon master responded.

Chapter Twenty-two

Home Dangerous Home

Perhaps I should have stayed the night, Kidwell wondered as she turned the unfamiliar rental car onto the last leg of county road heading to her house. She opened the window, letting the rush of cool air revive her exhausted mind and body. It had been a long journey, especially frustrating since Kidwell knew she need only take dragon form and be home in an instant. Too many people had seen her in the Netherlands. To suddenly disappear and reappear would be dangerous for the secret that must be kept, at least for now. Other protected despots needed to join the drug lord in the cells of the ICJ, something the secret would make possible. Kidwell felt her jacket pocket, assuring herself that the passport was still safely there. She didn't ask Roberto how he'd managed to obtain the Dutch entrance stamp that made possible her unquestioned exit from the country. It paid to have connections with the ICJ.

The journey home started with the flight from Amsterdam to Houston where she'd parted company with Aisha and Greg as they flew home to Lubbock and Kidwell headed for Albuquerque. It had been such a joy when the two joined her in Holland. For nearly two weeks, she'd stayed there, answering questions from the tiny group of ICJ attorneys with whom she and Roberto had shared their secret. It would be complicated during the trial, striving to explain how the international criminal had come to be a prisoner. In the end, a plan was made to provide sufficient evidence to ensure the court knew that releasing such information violated international security protocols. It was the best they could do. When it became apparent that Kidwell must remain in Holland, Aisha and Greg offered enthusiastically to join her, and with their arrival, it became a wonderful vacation. Kidwell's duties took little of her time, sometimes going two or three days between official meetings.

They drank beer just yards from where Heineken brewed their internationally respected beverage. Breakfast each day included a discussion of what museum to visit with more museums available than days to enjoy them. The Rijksmuseum was so huge it was overwhelming; Rembrandt's home made the artist come alive for Kidwell, and much the same for Van Gough when they visited that museum. They spent a whole day on a river tour, enjoying the amazing beauty of the Netherlands along the riverbanks, and they savored incredible food, Roberto and his wife frequently serving as their guide as they experienced the restaurants of The Hague and even Amsterdam.

The home of Anne Frank moved Kidwell more than any other place. Despite the jostling crowds, Kidwell couldn't stop staring at the actual diary where it rested in its glass case. When she'd first read the story as a teenager, she couldn't imagine spending days in silence, no interaction with the outside world. As she stood in the very place, it became all too real. During their stay, at least once each day, someone would recognize her or Aisha, from what they'd seen or heard about them and *The Book of Kidwell* and *The Book of Aisha*. The Anne Frank house was no exception.

Kidwell felt a gentle hand on her arm as she stood in one of the cramped rooms where the Franks' had hidden for so very long, the same room where the Nazis finally found them, dragging them away from their gentle, self-imposed prison to a human-made hell. She turned and considered the gentle blue eyes of a somewhat non-descript woman, dressed in a simple cotton dress, a purse hanging over her arm.

"My mother was a child in Dachau," the woman said, her English clear but with a hint of an accent that Kidwell could not recognize.

"I am so sorry at what was done to her, and so glad she lived to bring you into the world," Kidwell answered.

Tears teased at the woman's eyes, transforming them into a thing of beauty. "I have read your book," the woman said.

Kidwell took a deep breath, preparing to explain in her well-practiced speech that she would not do an autograph. She believed that doing so made it about her rather than the messages she'd been given.

"You won't let it happen again, will you?" the woman asked.

"What?"

"This," the woman said, waving her hand in an inclusive gesture of the home turned into a museum. "You won't let people do it again, will you?"

Kidwell couldn't breathe. She'd grown accustomed to the weight of what she and Aisha had been called to do. The woman's words brought it all back, like an elephant sitting on her chest.

"I'll do what I can," Kidwell said, tears now

dancing in her own eyes.

The woman raised a hand to stroke Kidwell's cheek gently. "Thank you," she said. She turned and stepped into a group of people, exiting the room and going into another. Kidwell would not see her again, but she would never forget her.

As she drove, Kidwell relived that moment, wondering, as she had so many times before, exactly what she should do to keep her promise to the woman. She knew it was something no one person could accomplish, but, as she promised, she would do what she could. It was a pledge she intended to keep.

Kidwell thought longingly of her own bed. True, it was only early evening in New Mexico, but her body had adjusted to Netherlands time, and she longed for sleep. She would have the place to herself. The last she'd spoken with Martin, she'd encouraged him to turn the horses out to pasture and go visit his family on the Apache reservation near Ruidoso. As much as she loved and appreciated the young man, she looked forward to the time alone. She had been around too many people for too long. She needed quiet.

The horses grazed happily in the pasture by the house as she turned down the driveway. She slowed, identifying and checking all five horses and the one mule, satisfying herself that they were content and not in need of her attention.

She parked the car in the empty yard, near the kitchen door. She sighed deeply as she looked around the familiar yard, smiling at not only the sights but also the smells of pine and hay and horse. She was home. Kidwell took the small duffle, her only luggage, containing the clothes and toiletries she'd purchased to make her Netherlands stay possible. As she walked up the back steps, she pulled keys from her pocket, one of the few items she'd pocketed before transforming to dragon, assuring access to essential items when she returned to human. She started to put the key in the lock, and the door drifted open.

Martin's not usually that careless, she thought just before she noticed the splintered wood where the deadbolt had once been secured in the doorframe. Dropping the bag, she turned to run, but not before a huge man jumped from behind the propane tank to block her way and another slammed the entry door open and grabbed her by the hair. Kidwell stabbed at the hand with her keys, drawing blood and issuing a Spanish curse from the man. The grip loosened, and for a second she was free, jumping off the steps and heading for the barn at a dead run before two men tackled her, one from the back and another from the side. She went down hard and struggled to breathe as the air was forced from her lungs. *Exhale, don't inhale*, she thought, remembering a long-ago lesson from Navy training when she fell at an obstacle course. Painfully, her lungs began to work again, hampered as she was dragged backwards into the house, and forced into a kitchen chair. She tried to focus, willing herself into dragon form, but a backhand blow to her face nearly knocked her unconscious, making her unable to concentrate. She struggled to gather her thoughts, looking around her and blowing at the blood that dribbled from her nose into her mouth. Two men, both armed with handguns, were already in the kitchen. The two who had tackled her stood beside her, holding her in the chair.

"What the hell?" she yelled.

"*Cerra la boca,*" a voice yelled. "How did you do

it?" the man continued, bending low, his angry face only inches from her own. "How did you take our *patron?*"

With the clarity of crisis, Kidwell realized that her captors' curiosity might be the only reason she was still alive.

"What are you talking about?" she demanded.

"You know," the man yelled; his breath held the hint of beans and chili, easy to discern as he breathed into her face. "How did you take our *patron* to those *pendejos* in Europe?"

"You must be crazy. How could I do that?" Kidwell asked. She saw a flicker of doubt cross his face. He stood straight, thinking.

He's just one of the goons, Kidwell thought. *Must take a lot of effort to think. I need to make him work harder at it.*

"Why do you think it was me?" she asked.

"You do strange things. You escaped the *serpientes*. You disappeared." His brow furrowed in thought. "And you were there, where he's in prison."

Kidwell sought to think fast though her head ached, keep him questioning. "Of course I was. They wanted to hear what I learned of his crimes while I was in your country."

In the distance, there was a sound of sirens. Her captors didn't notice.

The man stood thinking, wondering about her answer. Kidwell focused on the distant wail of sirens. *Please let them be coming here,* she prayed. He didn't think nearly long enough for Kidwell.

He shook his head. "It doesn't matter. We should have killed you when the *patron* told us to." He put his hand on the revolver in his waistband and pulled it free. Kidwell looked into his eyes and felt an odd sense of peace. She remembered the woman at the Anne Frank house. *I'm so sorry*, she thought. *I won't be able to keep my promise.* The sirens were growing louder but still too far away.

That was when the head of a bronze-tipped arrow appeared protruding through the man's chest and his blood spattered in Kidwell's face. She saw the surprise on his face as the life slipped from his body. Surprise also loosened the grip of the hands that held her, and she lunged up and forward, breaking free, at the same time grabbing for the pistol in the dying man's now flaccid grip. She heard the twang of a bowstring and the thud of an arrow hitting its mark. One of the men who held her grunted and clutched at his chest where an arrow now protruded, almost the full length of the shaft disappearing inside his body. As the first man fell, Kidwell could see clearly into the doorway leading to the living room. There stood a woman, tall and terrifying, clad in leather with a form fitted bronze breastplate and deep auburn hair bound in a braid down her back. Kidwell almost recognized her but not quite, surprised at the depth of joy she felt at the sight.

She's beautiful, Kidwell thought, despite the chaos around her. In that same instant, she saw another man across the kitchen as he leveled a pistol at the auburn-haired woman. Firing more with instinct than aim, Kidwell pulled the trigger on the pistol in her hand, hitting the man with a glancing shot across the front of his chest. It was non-fatal, but enough to throw off his aim so that his bullet hit a kitchen cabinet instead of the woman. In a flash, the warrior-woman pulled a sword from her belt and lashed out. The man's pistol fell to the ground along with his hand. He screamed and fell to his knees, fixating on the bloody stump of his arm. The sirens wailed just outside, coming to an abrupt stop, and Kidwell heard gunfire from the yard.

"*Madre de Dios,*" said the second man who had held Kidwell.

Until that moment, he'd stood transfixed, watching it all. His words brought him out of his shock, and he grabbed Kidwell with his left hand and reached for a pistol in a holster at his belt with his right. Kidwell elbowed him as hard as she could with an upward thrust toward his nose. He fell forward, hitting the edge of the kitchen table as he fell. Kidwell rolled him over, roughly, pointing the pistol at him as she did so. It was then she realized his only motion was an occasional twitch, more of nerve action than volition. She looked at his face. His nose was little more than a squashed piece of flesh. Kidwell felt sick as she realized the truth of it. A Navy Seal had taught her the move, and she was horrified to realize how easily it had worked. The man was dead, the septum of his nose now lodged in his brain.

Kidwell turned to the strange woman. Recognition hit hard.

"Maolan," she said.

"Yes," the woman answered. "Two of the four, together again, my dearest friend."

The gunfire outside had stopped. The bleeding man fainted, falling to the floor as the kitchen door burst open. A tall black man, folded over in a crouch, rushed inside, an automatic .45 held before him. He wore a black bulletproof vest with "FBI" emblazoned on the left breast and the back. As he assessed the situation, he rose, lowering his firearm to point at the floor.

Kidwell's brain shifted into another mode, and she reached in a kitchen drawer, withdrawing a tea towel, crossed to the unconscious man, and quickly made a tourniquet around his bleeding wrist.

The FBI agent checked the bodies of the other men, confirming that they were dead.

"Any others?" he asked.

"No," Maolan answered.

"There are two more outside. One dead, one injured. My partner is taking care of him," he turned to Kidwell. "Not the best of circumstances, but I'm pleased to meet you, Commander Brown."

"I'm certainly glad you're here," Kidwell answered.

"You're bleeding," he said.

Kidwell felt gently at her bloody nose. "I don't think it's broken. Just bruised."

The agent then turned to Maolan. "No offense intended, but who the hell are you?" He paused. "Again, no offense, but what the hell are you?"

Kidwell and Maolan looked at each other. "Uh…" Kidwell said.

The man looked back and forth between them. "Long story?" he asked.

"About ten thousand years long," Maolan answered.

Kidwell cleared her throat. "Would it bear any weight if I told you that it's important to national – no – to international security that the world not know she exists?"

The man looked a long time at Kidwell, then at Maolan. "My name's Walt Chandler," he said to Kidwell. "You don't know me, but I was assigned to find you a few years ago to learn if you were a threat to the nation." He paused, took a deep breath. "My partner and I never told anyone, but both our dead granddaddies came to us and told us to leave you alone. That you had important work to do."

"And you did, leave me alone that is," Kidwell said.

"My granddaddy was always right." He looked at Maolan. "You got a place to go?"

Kidwell and Maolan both laughed. "Aye," Maolan answered, her voice heavily accented with the sound of Ireland.

"Then go, before State Police and the paramedics get here," he said.

Maolan picked up her bow and turned to rush up the stairs, up to the dragon eye, her pathway back to dragon life.

Walt Chandler knelt and looked at the bronze arrowhead, peeking from the dead man's chest.

"How the hell are we going to explain that?" he asked.

"With as much of the truth as we can tell," Kidwell answered. "It was a miracle appearance. That's true. People are rather used to hearing about miracles from me."

The FBI agent stood at his full height and looked at her. "Yes, ma'am. I suppose they are."

Chapter Twenty-three

Full Circle

Kidwell figured it had been more than twenty-four hours since she last enjoyed the soft comfort of a bed. It had taken hours for the FBI, State Police, and paramedics to remove bodies, haul off the injured, and collect evidence. Kidwell had considered calling Martin, but she knew he would start immediately for home, and she didn't want him making the six-hour drive through the night. The danger was past. She was safe but shaken.

The kitchen and much of the yard were marked off with crime scene tape, but Agent Chandler had arranged that she be allowed to stay home, to sleep in her own bed. Once they'd cleared the house, even as police still photographed and gathered evidence in the yard, Kidwell had gone upstairs, stripped out of her blood and travel-stained clothing, and taken a long, hot bath. Chandler had also allowed her to fill an icepack from the kitchen refrigerator, and she held it gently on her bruised nose. She slipped into clean pajamas and collapsed across the bed, not yet finding the energy to climb under the covers. That was when she heard more than saw activity at the dragon eye. Flowing like liquid, Maolan appeared, standing before her. No longer dressed for war, she wore a soft, silk tunic and breeches of the same material, both a green much like the color of her dragon scales. Her full auburn hair now flowed freely. The woman stood, looking first at Kidwell, her eyes soft with concern. Then she glanced at both her hands.

"It feels odd to be human again," she said.

"I was terrified when I first saw my own dragon hand," Kidwell answered.

"But you didn't yet have the memories. I do."

Kidwell patted the bed beside her. Maolan sat down, and Kidwell grasped her hand, surprising herself at how easily she did so.

"I still have trouble grasping the relationship of, well, of all four of us," Kidwell said.

"It was a love like no other," Maolan answered. "We were family and more. Even, even Annalome. There is no bond equal to that of dragon and rider, and, somehow, perhaps because of your love of your brother, that bond extended to all four of us. We were almost one."

Kidwell sat up, taking both of Maolan's hands in her own. "And now we are only two. I'm not sure what that means."

Maolan softly touched Kidwell's face. "Don't you?" She took Kidwell's hand and gently pulled her to her feet.

Tears trickled down Kidwell's cheeks. Maolan brushed the tears away and then leaned close to kiss Kidwell gently on the lips. Kidwell was amazed at her reaction to that kiss. She felt a passion that went beyond the physical; it even succeeded in paling what she had felt with Anna, something she had not thought possible.

They worked together to pull back the covers, both slipping between the cool sheets. As they held each other, exchanging gentle kisses, Kidwell felt complete, exhausted but complete. In the end, that exhaustion ruled the night and they each slipped into sleep, a sleep made deeper because, for the first time in millennia, they were not alone.

❧❧❧❧

Anna shivered in the cool of the mountain night. She sat atop the hood of her truck where it was parked along a mountain road, the road that led to the cell tower that served the area. Binoculars held before her eyes, she watched the house and yard below, the place that had been the home she shared with Kidwell. A cry choked her as she watched the shadows in an upstairs window, the bedroom she had shared with the love of her life. She told herself she should not watch, but she couldn't stop. She saw the shadows move together, the forms of two women embracing, the light behind them. When the light went out, she could see no more.

Anna wept. The finality of it, of her total loss of Kidwell, weighed on her very soul, leaving her with a grief unlike any she had ever known. She had sat there most of the day, needing to know that Kidwell was safe. She had arrived just after the FBI stormed into the yard. She watched the gunfight between them and the drug lord lackeys. The hours had been almost unbearable as she waited for some sign of Kidwell's fate. Her relief was almost orgasmic when she finally saw Kidwell step outside, standing beside the FBI vehicle, apparently answering questions.

"She's alive, and she doesn't look hurt," she whispered to herself. Anna told herself she had seen what she needed to see, that it was time to go, but still she stayed, not really knowing why. Several times, she had nearly climbed back in her car, headed down the road and back to her old home, striving for the courage to see Kidwell again, to let her know how relieved she was to know that Kidwell was alive and well. She longed for Kidwell to know that it was her, Anna, who had forewarned the FBI. Even now, she was unsure if it was wisdom or lack of courage that kept her rooted to the hilltop, watching and not joining the scene below.

I stayed too long, Anna thought, deeply regretting what she had just witnessed.

"I'm glad for you," Anna whispered. "You deserve to be loved and to love, Kidwell."

Finally, exhaustion overcame her. It was too dark to drive the narrow, dirt track back down the mountain safely. She had brought her sleeping bag, and Anna curled up in the bed of the truck, warm in the bag. She drank deeply from her water bottle and the sleep of grief and exhaustion came quickly.

She did not see the golden figure sitting on the toolbox, who turned to look at her with care and love.

"Have faith, little one," the figure whispered, unheard by the woman she guarded. "The tale will unfold as it should for all concerned."

About the Author

As a writer and consultant, Kayt C. Peck has worked with many diverse organizations over the years. She found wisdom in the words and lives of people of all colors, religious beliefs, sexual orientation, nationalities, and socio-economic classes. Her multi-cultural exposure heavily influenced the writing of *Kiva and the Mosque* and this sequel, *The Pyramid and the Painting*, and flavors almost all her work. Her life-long career as a writer has included working as a journalist, a public-affairs officer in the U.S. Naval Reserve, and as a grants expert, writing applications raising more than $30 million for worthy domestic and even international organizations. She has published five other novels, one biography, and written many plays, including being a two-time awardee in the Rocky Mountain Voices play competition and receiving a special award for Excellence in Play Writing at the American Association of Community Theatres Region VI 2015 finals. She has authored and published numerous articles, short stories, and poems. The first edition of *Kiva and the Mosque* and her novel, *Good Water*, were both finalists in the New Mexico/Arizona Book Awards. Today, she lives quietly in her cabin home in the mountains of northeastern New Mexico.

Other books by Kayt

Good Water- ISBN- 978-1-939062-87-1

The dry plains drew Judy Proctor like a bear to her den…or a moth to the flame. Ranching was her life. The sweat as she branded or "doctored" cattle…the howl of a coyote in the quiet, night air…half-frozen fingers as she cut the wire to loosen hay bales for hungry cattle scratching for survival in snow-covered land…all of the everyday existence on the ranch was her life.
It was where she belonged.
It was a lonely life.

She had tried to leave the ranch to join the "normal" existence of a talented young woman in the city, but it had never been home. When her parents were killed in an automobile accident, she returned to the family ranch as much because she needed it as it needed her. She faced a lonely life to be shared with no better company than Somegood and Useless, her cow dog and the mottled mutt that were her companions.

Kathleen Romero slipped into Judy's life unexpectedly. She came to the plains to write a story. Would she stay because of the real truth she found in the simple drama of husbanding land and animals?

Unfortunately, even wide-open spaces can be plagued by prejudice and closed-minds. As the two women struggle to know each other, they must also carve a place for themselves among the country-folk who have been Judy's friends and neighbors her entire life.

The Ladies Room - ISBN - 978-1-943353-09-3

A dream is housed in the dusty, unused storage room above the Pink Triangle, one of Amber, Texas' two gay bars. Journalist April Sims serves as the reluctant leader in making that dream a reality. Under her guidance an eclectic group of women build a safe place in a community where being a lesbian can be dangerous and difficult.

April meets Sophia Mendez, a local attorney, as she seeks legal guidance for members of the group. In meeting with the women of the Ladies' Room, Sophia finds herself dealing with personal as well as professional issues.

When a radical religious group levels an attack on the entire gay community, even to the the point of a vigilante attack on the Pink Triangle, the strength and unity of the women of The Ladies' Room will be tested to the core.

Only time will tell if the beauty of the dream can override the ugliness of a harsh reality.

Prairie Fire - ISBN – 978-1-943353-47-7

Judy and Kathleen were accepted, even loved, by their conservative ranching neighbors. Their world felt safe and secure...until...until prairie fire! The flames disrupted their lives, causing destruction and injury, but the community pulled together to face a common enemy. When Kathleen's unofficial "daughter" found herself homeless, Pookie joined that community, bringing to this simple world her black clothes and rebellious nature. Together, conservative and liberal, gay and straight, they were a community, ready to face fire itself. The surprise to them all was the unseen enemy from within, one that had the potential to destroy them all.

The Kiva and The Mosque - ISBN - 978-1-943353-85-9

In a troubled world, answers rarely come from where they are expected. The need for answers to save a troubled humanity forces Kidwell Brown and Aisha Sudda, two total strangers, into roles they never could have anticipated. Kidwell and her life-partner, Anna Montoya, live a quiet life in their mountain home until the day Kidwell is drawn to visit the ceremonial cave at Bandelier National Monument. Hundreds of miles away, Aisha Sudda Fletcher lives another quiet existence, along with her husband, Greg, until the day she is drawn to visit a garden beside a vandalized mosque.

On that day, both Kidwell and Aisha are chosen. These humble women soon learn that the time of prophets has not yet passed. During mystical moments, each woman is given a message – "Desert Lightning has no power" to Kidwell, and "The scimitar has no edge," to Aisha. They each pass along the message as instructed, neither realizing they have predicted important moments in world history.

Their mystical guides direct the women to "find their allies," and so the lives of Kidwell, Aisha, Anna and Greg are forever intertwined. They will face victory and exile, mystery and certainty.

In the end the very nature of humanity proves to be the world in which they must fight and survive.

As an unabashed advocate for the gay/lesbian/bisexual/transgendered community in places were being different was dangerous, Kayt honed her skill in standing her ground and doing the right thing. Her entertaining and thought-provoking novels offer readers a rich banquet of characters, settings and scenarios that leave us both satisfied and wanting more.

Best-selling author Anne Hillerman